Acting Edition

I0591577

Angry Fags

by Topher Payne

ISBN 978-0-573-70510-6

www.concordtheatricals.com
www.concordtheatricals.co.uk

FOR PRODUCTION INQUIRIES

UNITED STATES AND CANADA
info@concordtheatricals.com
1-866-979-0447

UNITED KINGDOM AND EUROPE
licensing@concordtheatricals.co.uk
020-7054-7298

Each title is subject to availability from Concord Theatricals Corp.,
depending upon country of performance. Please be aware that
ANGRY FAGS may not be licensed by Concord Theatricals Corp. in
your territory. Professional and amateur producers should contact the
nearest Concord Theatricals Corp. office or licensing partner to verify
availability.

MUSIC AND THIRD-PARTY MATERIALS USE NOTE

IMPORTANT BILLING AND CREDIT REQUIREMENTS

ANGRY FAGS was originally produced by 7 Stages (Heidi S. Howard, Artistic Director) in Atlanta, Georgia on February 23, 2013. The production was directed by Justin Anderson, with set design by Nadia Morgan, costume design by DeeDee Chmielewski, sound and lighting design by Kevin Frazier, video design by Casey Williams, and properties by Melissa DuBois. The assistant stage manager was Holly Bennett and the stage manager was Kat Tierney. The cast was as follows:

BENNETT	Jacob York
COOPER	Johnny Drago
HAINES	Melissa Carter
KIMBERLY	Suehyla El-Attar
ADAM	John Benzinger
MUSGROVE	Marcie Millard
PRESTON	Michael Henry Harris

A substantially revised version of the work faced its first audience, again at 7 Stages (Heidi S. Howard, Artistic Director) in Atlanta, Georgia as part of the Homebrew Series in November 2017. It was directed by Topher Payne. The stage manager was Esther Lang Reeves. The cast was as follows:

BENNETT	Jacob York
COOPER	Pat Young
HAINES	Stacy Melich
KIMBERLY	Emily Sams Brown
ADAM	Daniel Carter Brown
MUSGROVE	Tiffany Porter
PRESTON	Mary Shaw

CHARACTERS

BENNETT RIGGS – Thirties. Speechwriter for a state senator. Cautiously optimistic, affable. Conflicted.

COOPER HARLOW – Thirties. Bennett's roommate. Caustic, clever, unpredictable. A fancy badass.

SENATOR ALLISON HAINES – Forties. A former activist, now the only out lesbian in the Georgia State Senate. Pragmatic, thoughtful, flawed. A dedicated public servant now wondering what happens when she's no longer celebrated by the public.

KIMBERLY PHILLIPS – Thirties. The senator's office manager, a married mother of two. Good-humored, quick, overworked. Probably really enjoyed her early twenties.

ADAM LOWELL – Thirties. The senator's chief of staff. Undeniably appealing and charmingly square. Likely owns a lot of books about Bobby Kennedy.

PEGGY MUSGROVE – Forties. The senator's opponent. Genuine, witty, nimble. A black female Republican, with all the conflicts and potential advantages that implies. She's found a way to weaponize being othered.

DEIRDRE PRESTON – Fifties. A local broadcasting legend. Has the shrewd and discerning eye of a brilliant woman who believes her best days are still ahead of her.

SETTING

Atlanta

TIME

After Trump

A NOTE ON THE MEDIA WALL

Angry Fags incorporates the use of scripted video projections. When stage directions indicate a character is "on screen," these are intended to be pre-recorded segments. Although if you're inspired to find a way to innovate and do the media wall live, perhaps broadcasting in real time from another room, the author admires your ambition and wishes you well in your endeavor.

This play is dedicated to

Johnny Drago
and
Suehyla El-Attar

For their endless support of my storytelling,
and for making it better.

ACT ONE

Scene One

*(**COOPER** and **BENNETT** are on a hillside. A picnic basket is in front of them. They are both drinking red wine from plastic cups. A small cheese and cracker plate between them. **BENNETT** is eating pistachios.)*

COOPER. Time check.

BENNETT. It's five twenty-two.

COOPER. That a new watch?

BENNETT. Why yes it is.

COOPER. Snazzy.

BENNETT. Isn't it?

COOPER. Your old one die?

BENNETT. No.

COOPER. You got it wet and it died. You wore it in the bathtub, didn't you?

BENNETT. No. And that is an oddly specific accusation.

COOPER. No it's not. There's a pattern of behavior, Bennett. You spilled coffee on your laptop. Some sort of red sauce on that shirt you borrowed from me for your class reunion –

BENNETT. Never gonna live that down.

COOPER. And I'm sure there have been other sloshes and spills no one witnessed. But you know they happened. You have trouble with liquids. Be careful with that wine.

BENNETT. My old watch did not die. I left it at Sammy's. And after everything, I just thought there'd be a lot of unnecessary stress if I went back for it.

COOPER. Ah.

BENNETT. So I got a snazzy new watch.

COOPER. Could've had it mailed to you.

BENNETT. Nobody mails things anymore.

COOPER. Sure they do.

BENNETT. When's the last time you put something in the mail?

COOPER. Couple days ago. Netflix.

BENNETT. Why don't you just stream movies like a normal human?

COOPER. Netflix in the mailbox gives me something to look forward to. I'm certainly not expecting any letters. People used to write letters. Another lost art.

BENNETT. Which door is it?

COOPER. The one on the left. As I said before.

　　　　(He sips.)

I should write more letters.

BENNETT. I'd love to get a letter. Write me a letter, Cooper.

COOPER. We live in the same house. What would I say in a letter?

BENNETT. Next time you have a date –

COOPER. I don't date.

BENNETT. But the next time you *do*, don't tell me about it. Write it all down, slide it under my door. Then I'll read it and we'll talk about it.

COOPER. If I go to the trouble of writing you a letter, you're writing me back.

BENNETT. So we'll have the things we talk about, and the things we only write letters about?

COOPER. This sounds unnecessarily complex.

BENNETT. Pistachio?

COOPER. No. I do not support your newfound interest in pistachios. Sitting there with a pile of abandoned nut casings, stuffing your cheeks. You look like a chipmunk.

BENNETT. It's really heartbreaking that you're my best friend.

(They drink for a moment.)

Oh, shit, is that –

(He picks up binoculars and stands.)

COOPER. No, it's not. Sit down. You're jumpy.

BENNETT. Yeah, well. You're really going through that wine.

COOPER. I'm nervous, a little. Not bad nervous, more –

BENNETT. Anticipation?

COOPER. I think so. Like first date nervous.

BENNETT. Speaking of which, you talk to that volunteer from the office yet? David, right?

COOPER. Still avoiding him, but totally fantasizing. A Log Cabin Republican. That is a very complicated worldview, I don't know if I can take that on.

BENNETT. Your worldview is equally complex.

COOPER. To the contrary. My worldview is shockingly streamlined.

BENNETT. Sleeping with someone named David just sounds stable, solid. Biblical. I've slept with two Davids. Maybe three. Good people. You remember that line from *Steel Magnolias* about all gay men being named Mark, Rick, or Steve?

COOPER. Love that movie.

BENNETT. Me too. I don't think it's true anymore. Now they're all David, Ryan, or Chris.

COOPER. I know like eight Travises.

BENNETT. David, Ryan, or Travis. My aunt did *Steel Magnolias* at her community theater, few years back. The play's different. Whole thing's in the beauty shop. No hospital scenes, no bleeding armadillo groom's cake. I mean, they talk about it, but you never see it.

COOPER. Well that's not the same goddamn thing. That's why I don't go to plays. I always like the movie better.

BENNETT. Nothing replaces the live experience. It's one thing to see it on a screen, but having those emotions, that sense of immediacy, right there in the same room, it's amazing. The tiniest little action – smoking. When someone smokes in a movie, you see it. When someone smokes in a play, you *smell* it.

COOPER. But I don't like the smell of smoke.

BENNETT. Whether you enjoy it or not isn't the damn point. It's part of the world. You just have to deal with it. Everything's better live, because you can't get away from it. Total immersion.

COOPER. That's not better. That requires more involvement than I wanna sign up for. I saw *Hair* at some theater. Those fucking hippies came right up to my seat and sang in my face. This did not make it more *real* for me, because if someone did that in the *real* world, I would take my car keys and I would attack them.

BENNETT. I would enjoy seeing that.

COOPER. You try the cheese?

BENNETT. Nope. I'm suspicious. What's its name again?

COOPER. Lorraine.

BENNETT. That sounds made-up.

COOPER. Everything, at some point, was made up. Eat the goddamn cheese.

> (**BENNETT** *tries a delicate nibble, then makes an elaborate display of revulsion.*)

BENNETT. Muueehh. Mueeeeh. That's nasty. It tastes like Swiss.

COOPER. Oh, just stop it.

BENNETT. It tastes like sadness.

COOPER. Eat your fucking pistachios.

> (**BENNETT** *is satisfied. He returns to his pistachios.* **COOPER** *eats a hunk of cheese, defiantly, as a testament to its quality.*)

Mmmmm. Oh, I've got one. Action movies. You can't do action on stage.

BENNETT. Maybe not, but a car chase would be more exciting in person.

COOPER. This is true. Very exciting. Violence, mayhem, explosions.

BENNETT. But you don't like the smell of smoke.

COOPER. That's why you observe from a safe distance.

(*A little laugh, realizing.*)

You know who likes the smell of smoke?

BENNETT. Yes I do.

COOPER. Never see pictures of him smoking in public. Everybody's got their little secrets. Laura Bush smoked.

BENNETT. So did Obama.

COOPER. But nobody saw it. Sign of weakness.

BENNETT. That's so stupid. You can't just have a cigarette anymore without it *meaning* something.

COOPER. You miss it?

BENNETT. Every fucking day. It used to punctuate moments, you know? After a meal, after sex, the drive home from work. Those moments bleed together now. My life is a run-on sentence.

COOPER. Filthy habit.

BENNETT. To be certain.

COOPER. You smell better.

BENNETT. Thank you.

COOPER. How long now?

BENNETT. Forty-two days. I had my last one outside the police station the night everything went to hell.

COOPER. And you haven't cheated? Haven't snuck out for one with anybody from the office?

BENNETT. We're not talking about people from my office right now.

COOPER. That wasn't intentional.

BENNETT. You promised.

COOPER. I slipped.

BENNETT. Well, don't slip. Honor your promises.

(They snack in silence.)

BENNETT. I did think it'd be easier by now.

COOPER. What?

BENNETT. Quitting smoking.

COOPER. You can only change behavior. Not inclinations.

BENNETT. Shit, that's him!

COOPER. So it is.

> *(**COOPER** reaches into the picnic basket and takes out an inexpensive cell phone. They stand.)*

BENNETT. Wait.

COOPER. For what?

BENNETT. Let him get one good drag.

COOPER. You're a true humanitarian.

> *(They watch.)*

All those years of him going on TV, saying *we're* gonna burn.

BENNETT. Cooper. Do it. Now.

> *(**COOPER** presses a button. They wait. Nothing happens.)*

COOPER. Shit.

> *(He frantically presses the button.)*

BENNETT. Did you do it right?

COOPER. How would I know? I got the instructions online, you never know if that's reliable. They don't do user reviews for this sort of –

> *(An explosion. Deafening sound and a brilliant flash of light. **COOPER** and **BENNETT** are knocked backward, their faces now illuminated by the orange glow of unseen flames.)*

BENNETT. Jesus Christ.

COOPER. Wow. You were right, that was so much better than a movie.

> *(They watch, intrigued and horrified, as lights fade.)*

Scene Two

(Two months ago.)

(The media wall comes to life and we see Atlanta broadcasting legend **DEIRDRE PRESTON** *at her newsdesk.)*

PRESTON. The eyes of the country remain fixed upon Georgia District Fifty-Seven, as Senator Allison Haines heads into a runoff election against political newcomer Peggy Musgrove. Senator Haines was the featured speaker at today's Women's Leadership Conference at the Georgian Terrace Hotel. In her remarks, Haines made an appeal for unity.

> *(***SENATOR ALLISON HAINES***, giving a speech at a lectern. Supporters stand behind her – all women, all white.)*

HAINES. We are living in a time when we're capable of communicating with most anyone in the world in an instant. And yet, with all this newfound opportunity to connect, having a civil conversation seems to be increasingly beyond our grasp.

I believe the world isn't just getting smaller, it's getting *closer*. We can unite under that Gold Dome, to make a better future for every single citizen of the great state of Georgia. The only requirement is the will to work together. As for those who aren't willing? They're gonna find themselves on the wrong side of history.

> *(The image pauses. Lights up on* **HAINES** *in her office, holding a remote control. Seated before her are two of her staff members,* **ADAM** *and* **KIMBERLY***.)*

HAINES. Okay, pop quiz. Who can tell me what's wrong with this picture?

> *(A pause.)*

I presented as more confrontational than I intended. I will rephrase.

(A smile.)

Team. Is there anything on-screen which would prove instructive when planning future events?

KIMBERLY. You might want to re-think that jacket.

> *(***BENNETT*** *enters in business attire with a cup of coffee.)*

HAINES. What's wrong with the jacket?

BENNETT. It's a little Julia Sugarbaker.

HAINES. Duly noted.

ADAM. Who's Julia Sugarbaker?

BENNETT. You're kidding, right?

HAINES. Hey, squirrely-tails, focus. Look again. Is something *missing*? Behind me. This should be easy.

KIMBERLY. Everybody's white.

HAINES. Ten points to Kimberly! It looks like the Country Music Awards up there.

> *(She turns off the media wall.)*

Where my blacks at?

ADAM. Senator, seating on the dais was reserved for their senior leadership. In this instance, that was a bunch of white women.

HAINES. Well, that's a problem, isn't it? A Republican can win with nothing but white people. Democrats gotta appeal to literally *everyone else*. We can't afford these kind of optics, guys.

BENNETT. Senator, last time you had to court all the margins. Now you're the incumbent, you can run on your record.

HAINES. Please stop saying that. Everybody in the damn country is watching this race, and nobody gives a shit about my record.

ADAM. I wouldn't say that's –

HAINES. I'm a white lesbian up against a black female Republican. It's like they found a goddamn unicorn.

KIMBERLY. Plus she adopted that deaf baby.

HAINES. Yes, Kimberly, people love Peggy Musgrove's fucking adopted deaf baby. I'm so sick of – I get it, my kids have all five senses, so I'm not *brave* like Peggy Musgrove. She isn't brave! She picked it out! I mean good for her, but it's not like it was a surprise.

BENNETT. Can I please put that in a press release?

HAINES. Do not try to make me laugh, Bennett, I am immune to your charms today. I need my shoes.

KIMBERLY. Got 'em.

> (**KIMBERLY** *hands her a pair of high heels.* **HAINES** *kicks off her sneakers and puts them on.)*

HAINES. Adam, tell Senator Newsome I need to see his numbers before I give support on SR 151, and he knows me well enough to expect that. Bennett, email me the revisions on the speech for the prayer breakfast, I'll look over it tonight. Kimberly, tomorrow afternoon when I cut the ribbon on that Habitat for Humanity house, it'd better look like a Tyler Perry movie behind me.

> (**HAINES** *exits.)*

KIMBERLY. If y'all will excuse me, I've gotta rustle up some ladies in church hats. Anybody got a vaguely Asian contact who's free tomorrow?

ADAM. Believe it or not, I do. The president of my condo association looks just like John Cho. I'll call him.

KIMBERLY. You're my hero.

ADAM. Anybody up for a beer after we get outta here?

KIMBERLY. I can't. Stupid husband. Stupid children.

ADAM. Bennett?

BENNETT. I shouldn't. I've been living out of boxes the last two weeks. My roommate is threatening to set them on fire. Cooper says it's like living in a shanty town.

ADAM. I could give you a hand. I can organize a bookshelf like you wouldn't believe.

BENNETT. Is that a fact?

ADAM. My secret is arranging by color. Gives it visual appeal.

BENNETT. I'll try that out.

ADAM. Shit, now you don't need me. Never should've told you my secret.

BENNETT. Well, remember that for next time. Know when to keep a few secrets.

ADAM. I'll take note of that.

(**ADAM** *exits.*)

KIMBERLY. You have sex with him right now.

BENNETT. No. We work together. I'm not gonna date someone I work with.

KIMBERLY. I did not say date. I said have sex with him.

BENNETT. I should probably get the ruins of my last relationship unpacked before I pick another guy to mess with my head.

KIMBERLY. Fine. Stay home, unpack, lick your wounds. When you're ready, I'll have a list of people for you to sleep with on my behalf. So far it's Adam and the fella at the Starbucks kiosk.

BENNETT. The blonde guy with the Celtic knot on his wrist?

KIMBERLY. (*Taking cigarettes from her purse.*) Yes indeed.

BENNETT. I have a rule against stupid tattoos. It indicates a lack of regard for long-term consequences.

KIMBERLY. You are such a waste of gay.

BENNETT. Ooh, I'm smoking.

KIMBERLY. No, you're quitting.

BENNETT. Yes I am. But I get to have cigarettes for the first week I'm on the pill. And then, presumably, I will wake up tomorrow and have no desire to smoke again. So tomorrow should be a red-letter day.

(**KIMBERLY** *and* **BENNETT** *exit.*)

Scene Three

(The media wall comes to life, with **PRESTON** *appearing again, this time in a one-on-one with* **PEGGY MUSGROVE**. *They're at a kitchen table. The lighting is soft and flattering.)*

MUSGROVE. I certainly didn't expect this, Deirdre. But I've lived the frustration of being Allison Haines's constituent.

PRESTON. How was it frustrating?

MUSGROVE. We see her on CNN talking about gay adoption, on MSNBC talking about Planned Parenthood...really the only place we never see her is in District Fity-Seven. Someone has to step forward and do the job Allison Haines has spent two years ignoring in favor of her own agenda.

PRESTON. So gay adoption, reproductive rights, those are outside of a state senator's purview?

MUSGROVE. See, Deirdre, a question like that can be so insidious. Because we should be talking about why our schools are failing. We should discuss why our public transportation is so woefully subpar that citizens won't even use it when an interstate highway collapses. But I watch TV. If you can get a sound bite out of me on some contentious concept, it'll be the only thing you run. Well, I'm very sorry, but I won't be participating in that.

PRESTON. But these "contentious concepts" do impact the constituents you'd be serving.

MUSGROVE. And if a piece of legislation emerged on one of those issues, I'd talk to the good people of my district, find out what represents their interests, and their values. We've seen what happens when we give this job to someone with their own agenda. My desire is to be a voice for my friends and neighbors.

PRESTON. Even when the will of the people doesn't match your personal beliefs?

MUSGROVE. Especially when that happens, because then I'll know I'm doing my job.

*(Bennett and Cooper's house is revealed. We see the living room and kitchen counter. A hallway leads off. The furnishings are modern. Tasteful. A little cold. **BENNETT** is in gym shorts and a t-shirt, unpacking a box of dishes while watching the interview. He turns off the television.)*

BENNETT. Oh man. We're gonna lose so bad.

*(**COOPER** enters, dressed for a night out, a little buzzed.)*

COOPER. Ask me what happened.

BENNETT. What happened?

COOPER. I can't tell you.

BENNETT. Alright.

COOPER. Don't you *dare* leave it at that, you filthy faggot.

BENNETT. If you've been sworn to silence –

COOPER. It's just, he begged me. Begged me. "Please," he pleaded. "Don't tell Bennett."

BENNETT. Someone said that specifically.

COOPER. Yes.

BENNETT. Who?

COOPER. I can't tell you.

BENNETT. What was it regarding?

COOPER. Very bad behavior.

BENNETT. Where?

COOPER. At the bar.

BENNETT. Naturally.

COOPER. It was tragic. There were witnesses. People hung their heads in empathetic shame.

BENNETT. I am not interested in tragic bar behavior. If I were interested, I would go to bars, and witness tragic bar behavior.

COOPER. You are such a class act. I hope I'm classy when I'm as old as you.

BENNETT. We're eight months apart.

COOPER. I know, but from the looks of you, it was a very hard eight months.

(His phone rings. He looks.)

It's Lance. I'll call him back. Did you have a good night?

BENNETT. Yeah, fuckin' Peggy Musgrove did this interview where she was sidestepping every –

COOPER. I've already lost interest. I am spent. You just focus on your dishware and never give my little story a second thought.

BENNETT. That will not be difficult.

COOPER. *(As he heads for the hall.)* I suppose it doesn't matter that it was your ex-boyfriend.

BENNETT. Get the fuck back in here!

COOPER. *(Reeling back in.)* Okay, so I'm at the bar with the boys –

BENNETT. Which boys?

COOPER. Lance and his stupid friend Coby, you know with the scarves? And who do I see across the room, in his Merona shirt and khakis from Target, but your former paramour Mister Sammy Garrison. He is shitcanned on tequila sunrises and it's not even nine o'clock.

BENNETT. Yeah, that tracks.

COOPER. So. I don't think much of him, 'cause I never did, and Lance and I listen to Coby seriously talk for twenty minutes about whether it's okay for him to wear bronzing powder, I am not making that up.

BENNETT. Why does Lance hang out with him?

COOPER. I will never know. So, *then*. This guy comes in – he's got that floppy undercut that's like Justin Timberlake 2014 or current white supremacist?

BENNETT. I know this haircut.

COOPER. And the guy's creepy, but the raw materials are okay, it's all self-sabotage, like he went to the sale section at Urban Outfitters and intentionally made all the worst choices. And he's scanning the room with this look of like, hungry, needy, desperation. Like if he had this look at a Chuck E. Cheese, he would go to jail.

BENNETT. So, closet case from out of town.

COOPER. Closet case from out of town, precisely. And with his serial killer glasses and the top button done up on his chambray, we can't tell if he's a hipster or a sociopath –

BENNETT. Such a fine line.

COOPER. I know, right? But the trousers are always the giveaway.

BENNETT. I love that you say trousers.

COOPER. Skinny stretch? Harmless hipster. Dad jeans? Potential mass murderer. And this guy? Total Dad jeans. High-rise, pancake butt. Stranger danger.

(*His phone rings again. He answers.*)

Not now, Lance, I'm telling Bennett the story.

(*He hangs up.*)

Where was I?

BENNETT. You were describing his trousers and started spiraling.

COOPER. Right. Right. So, Closet Case in Dad Jeans orders a Bud Light, because *of course he did*, and guess who was suddenly on him like white on rice?

BENNETT. Ew!

COOPER. Yes! And he was a drunk *mess*, Bennett. Sammy was like, flopping on the bar, crawling all over this guy, sayin', "I sure do love me a clean-cut hunk of man." Those words actually came out of his mouth.

BENNETT. When Sammy gets drunk he talks like Paula Deen.

COOPER. This goes on for a while. Dad Jeans is all, "You like baseball?" And Sammy's all, "Sure I do!"

BENNETT. He does not!

COOPER. And then Sammy wants another "Teee-keeela Sunriiise," but the bartender, new, cute, I didn't get a name, he cuts Sammy off. And Sammy. Loses. His. Mind. Just takes to screamin' and sobbin' about how everybody hates him and he'll die alone, and the new bartender is at a loss, so he says it's time for him to go. And Dad Jeans offers to take him home! So he gets escorted out, in tears, with Dad Jeans, and as he passes me he looks up, mortified, and says, "Pleeease, don't tell Bennett."

BENNETT. That is the greatest story I have ever heard. Ever.

COOPER. I stayed for about three more hours, but that's really where the night peaked.

> (**COOPER**'s *phone rings again.*)

BENNETT. He's just going to keep calling.

COOPER. Jesus!

> (*He answers.*)

Bennett agrees. Best story ever.

> (*A lengthy pause.*)

Oh my god.

BENNETT. What now?

> (**COOPER** *shushes him.*)

What?

COOPER. (*Into phone.*) Who? Where?

BENNETT. Stop asking non-descriptive questions!

COOPER. Thanks, honey. Be safe.

> (*He hangs up.*)

One of the barbacks was out dumping the trash. They found Sammy behind the dumpster. Somebody beat the shit out of him with a baseball bat.

> (*Blackout.*)

Scene Four

(Police station. Sounds of activity all around.
KIMBERLY, **BENNETT**, *and* **COOPER** *sit in a row*
of chairs, each engaged with their respective
phones.)

COOPER. This environment is intolerable. This should be the place they take people when they're accused of crimes, but witnesses and victims can go someplace nicer. It wouldn't be that hard for them to maintain. You walk in a place like this, you feel like you're guilty of something.

BENNETT. Sammy's sister says his parents are driving in. I feel weird. Should I call them? We always got along okay.

KIMBERLY. You can call them after they catch the asshole who did this.

*(**ADAM** enters with cups of coffee for everyone.)*

ADAM. This coffee has the consistency of chocolate syrup, just so you're warned. Has anybody come back to talk to you?

KIMBERLY. Yes, but they just told us not to leave. And then went away.

BENNETT. Really, you guys, it's great of you to come down, but I just called Adam to get the name of the community liaison. It's late, you should all go get some sleep.

KIMBERLY. Don't be stupid. We've known Sammy for years. Just because you two ended your relationship doesn't change our concern for him. And I'm sure it doesn't change yours.

BENNETT. No. It doesn't.

KIMBERLY. They'll catch whoever did this. Allison won't let up. This is one of those times when you need a really stubborn lesbian.

BENNETT. That's true.

*(**HAINES** enters, wearing a college sweatshirt and jeans, looking surprisingly ordinary.)*

ADAM. Find out anything?

HAINES. Yes. Sergeant Levinson is on leave. Her mother had a stroke. Kimberly, we should send a card.

BENNETT. So who's the community liaison while she's out?

HAINES. There isn't one.

BENNETT. Shit.

COOPER. Why's that bad?

BENNETT. The guy picked Sammy because he was gay. So it's a hate crime.

HAINES. Well, technically no. Not according to Georgia law.

BENNETT. But according to *federal* law it is. Or did that go away with Obama too?

KIMBERLY. I'm not sure what rights we have today, someone check Twitter.

COOPER. So, what? We call the FBI?

BENNETT. If it comes to that.

ADAM. First we see how this plays out with the police.

HAINES. But before you talk to whatever random detective the APD is going to assign, I need the specifics on what happened.

BENNETT. Why?

HAINES. Because it's very important to be thorough right now. Cooper, what'd the guy look like?

COOPER. White guy. Mid-thirties, maybe? I don't know. Alt-Right haircut, Dad jeans. Serial killer glasses.

HAINES. Serial killer glasses?

COOPER. You know, like the guy who shot John Lennon and Ronald Reagan?

KIMBERLY. Those were two different people.

COOPER. No shit, seriously?

ADAM. Could your friends from the bar help?

COOPER. No, Lance couldn't see because he was wearing sunglasses. In a bar. At night. And his stupid friend Coby is...stupid. They should talk to the new bartender.

ADAM. What's his name?

COOPER. I only learn their names when they give me free drinks.

HAINES. So we know Sammy was drunk –

COOPER. Oh yeah.

HAINES. Is it possible anything else was going on there?

BENNETT. Meaning?

HAINES. Recreational drug use. I'm not judging.

BENNETT. He drinks. He buys pot from his cousin.

COOPER & KIMBERLY. Tyler.

BENNETT. Everybody buys from Tyler.

HAINES. I'm concerned.

BENNETT. About?

HAINES. They could say this was drug-related.

BENNETT. That's not what this was.

COOPER. This was a twisted creep who lured him out of the bar to beat the shit out of him.

HAINES. But you have to look at –

> *(A text message alert.)*

KIMBERLY. It's mine.

> *(**KIMBERLY** consults her phone.)*

HAINES. Look at what can be proven, because everyone else is going to.

ADAM. If it was obvious he was in danger, why did you let him leave?

COOPER. I didn't think Sammy was in danger.

ADAM. Then what did you think?

COOPER. I don't know, that he'd get crabs, or the guy would show him pictures of his favorite Confederate monuments or some shit.

Sammy cheated on my best friend, and now he was at a bar, blackout drunk and miserable, going home with some flat-ass closet case. So yeah, I didn't stop it because I thought they deserved each other.

KIMBERLY. Adam, somebody tipped off Eyewitness News that the senator's here. Deirdre Preston is on her way.

ADAM. Deirdre Preston is an anchor. She doesn't do remotes in the middle of the night.

KIMBERLY. Apparently tonight she does.

HAINES. Shit.

> (**HAINES** *immediately goes to her purse, pulls a makeup bag.*)

ADAM. Bennett, can you –

BENNETT. Right. Grab a pen. Ahhh, it is a tragedy when any act of violence…is perpetrated against one of our fellow citizens… One of our fellow citizens, particularly when that act is borne out of hatred and misunderstanding –

HAINES. Wait, back it up, back it up. We don't know that. We know Sammy was drunk, possibly high, obviously pursuing casual sex –

BENNETT. So he deserved to get his face bashed in?

HAINES. Of course not! But we are less than two months from the runoff, Bennett. Do you know why Deirdre Fucking Preston is out there at four in the morning? Because she knows this is the kind of salacious bullshit that can blow up a political career, and she's just itching to light the fuse. So we can – we can make a general statement of support while maintaining a safe distance, until we know more.

BENNETT. We can't abandon Sammy just because he wasn't assaulted under the best possible circumstances!

HAINES. We're not abandoning him. There is a way to focus attention on the larger issue of the attack without getting mired in details which may prove problematic later. Not just for us, but for Sammy as well.

BENNETT. You know, statements like that really make people hate politicians. I thought you came here tonight because you actually gave a shit about Sammy.

HAINES. I do. You know that.

BENNETT. 'Til you find out he doesn't make for very good TV. Don't worry, we're demonized so constantly, there's bound to be another bashing real soon, maybe the next victim will have a better narrative.

ADAM. Bennett, stop talking.

BENNETT. How the hell did you get so cynical right in front of me? You're embarrassing. You're gross. And fuck the damn magic pills, I'm having a cigarette.

(**BENNETT** *exits as lights fade.*)

Scene Five

(Media wall: We see a snapshot of Sammy, recent. Then **PRESTON** *reporting in a parking lot near a dumpster, in early-morning hours. Crime scene tape.)*

PRESTON. What we *do* know is that shortly before one this morning, thirty-three-year-old Samuel Garrison was found here, behind this dumpster, by an unnamed bar employee. The assailant, at large. The weapon?

(Brandishes a baseball bat.)

A baseball bat, like this one. Atlanta Police will not confirm or deny whether Garrison was targeted due to his close ties with the office of District Fifty-Seven State Senator Allison Haines. I spoke with the senator earlier this morning.

*(***HAINES*** stands at the entrance to a police station. She has been styled.)*

HAINES. The victim was a volunteer on my first campaign. I was made aware of the assault by a member of my staff. I have every faith in the brave men and women of the Atlanta Police Department, and I am confident his assailant will be apprehended and brought to justice.

(The media wall goes black. **BENNETT** *is on the sofa, holding a remote control. He's a little drunk.* **COOPER** *is refilling beers from a growler.)*

BENNETT. Booo! Motherfucker. She didn't even say his *name*, Cooper.

COOPER. I know, the beer is coming.

BENNETT. Sammy stuffed envelopes for that bitch! Thousands!

COOPER. The beer will help. I can put a Percocet in it.

BENNETT. No, that's okay.

COOPER. Alright, well I put one in mine and now I'm not sure which is which.

BENNETT. She can't even say his fucking name.

COOPER. Sammy is toxic, haven't you heard? I told you that for years, but now even senators know it.

BENNETT. Don't make Sammy jokes. Not right now.

COOPER. I'm sorry, but if I can't make fun of Sammy, even in a time of crisis, the terrorists have won.

BENNETT. That's what it is, isn't it? These aren't hate crimes, it's fucking terrorism. Fanatics who will beat us, try to kill us in the streets, and for what? Because I like boys. How is that hurting anybody? What's so wrong with us?

COOPER. No no no, you see what you're doing there? That's the same poor fuckin' pitiful faggot crap that makes us such an easy target. "Please, won't you accept me? I'm just like you!" You know what? I have seen The People of Walmart. I am *not* just like them.

BENNETT. And why do those fuckers get to be in charge anyway, huh? I mean, the Bible's a fine book with many good stories –

COOPER. Best-selling book of all time.

BENNETT. But what sane person bases their existence on a two-thousand-year-old instruction manual? I don't run round saying, "Hold up, before I make a major decision lemme consult the Epic of Gilgamesh."

COOPER. You're so well-read.

BENNETT. They're gonna come at us saying they occupy some moral high ground when they all voted for Donald Fucking Trump?

COOPER. They'd rather blow up the world than lose their power. That's why they always win. We won't accept a suicide mission. They absolutely will.

BENNETT. And even the people who try to empower us are still fucking apologists. The whole "It Gets Better" thing? It was a sweet sentiment, but *come on.* It gets better, unless you're fired from your job, or can't rent an apartment. It gets better, unless you get fat, because the gay community will make you feel invisible. It gets

better, depending on where you live and how honest
you want to be. Fuck all that. The message should have
been "Make it better."

COOPER. Hell yes. If you want to live in a better world, then
fucking take your piece of it. Make it better!

BENNETT. I'm so tired of trying to be likeable! It is
exhausting! Real change doesn't come from them
liking us. That's not how it happened for women, or
black people, or the founding of this fucking country.
Change doesn't happen because the majority has warm
fuzzy feelings about you. It happens because they see
you're not going to back down, and they get scared of
the consequences.

COOPER. Change doesn't come from reason. It comes from
fear.

BENNETT. And no one is afraid of us. Not really. Gay men
aren't seen as men.

COOPER. Because we don't *act* like men. We are part of a
tribe, goddamn it. It is part of our elemental instinct as
humans with dicks to protect our *tribe*.

BENNETT. Fuck yes! Protect the fucking tribe! We suck.
I'll say it, I'll admit it. Gay people suck at defending
ourselves, and we suck at taking care of each other.

COOPER. I brought you a possibly Percocet-laced beer at
nine in the morning!

BENNETT. Fine. You rock. But I hate everybody else.

COOPER. I feel the same way. Let's head over to Walmart
and get ourselves some discount weapons, start taking
these fuckers out.

BENNETT. There's a gun in my nightstand, I'm good to go.

COOPER. Whoa. Record scratch. There's a gun in my house?

BENNETT. There's a gun in *my room*.

COOPER. You own a handgun?

BENNETT. I'm from Alabama, of course I own a handgun.
My dad gave it to me when I moved to Atlanta. Stop
clutching your pearls.

COOPER. This is new and shocking information. Why exactly do you have it?

BENNETT. For protection.

COOPER. No, darling. I have a taser for protection. Somewhere. I think it's in my car. A gun is not for protection, it's for putting holes in various people and things, and that's just tacky, I'm sorry. Now I'm worried you're gonna start dispensing vigilante justice like Jodie Foster in that movie.

BENNETT. *The Accused*?

COOPER. I was thinking of *The Brave One*.

BENNETT. Could also have been *Panic Room*. Or that movie where her kid goes missing on the airplane.

COOPER. Jodie Foster's really dealing with some demons. I hope she's feeling better now.

BENNETT. I'm sure she is, *because she's part of the tribe*! She's owning it!

COOPER. Lesbians are a different tribe. Bisexuals. Trans people. The tribes are complimentary, perhaps, but distinct.

BENNETT. I disagree. I think we're all one tribe.

COOPER. No. Trans guys are their own tribe, Bennett. Thousands of men don't all decide to name themselves "Aiden" without a community supporting it.

BENNETT. Okay, but don't you think we're stronger if we all band together?

COOPER. Maybe! Who the hell knows? We can't even agree on a presidential candidate when the alternative is setting the goddamn world on fire.

BENNETT. But we did the Women's March. That was a good day.

COOPER. Yeah, sure, we'll play defense, but never offense. We will never unite like the other side does, you know why?

BENNETT. Because it's easier to get idiots to play follow the leader.

COOPER. Ding ding. Our side thinks too much. We pick everything to shreds if it isn't perfect.

BENNETT. And perfect is the enemy of good.

COOPER. That is profound.

BENNETT. It's not mine.

COOPER. I never know when you're quoting.

BENNETT. I know.

COOPER. You own a gun.

BENNETT. Yes. Do you want me to get rid of it?

COOPER. I can't decide. I just never pictured having a gun in my house.

BENNETT. You gonna keep calling this *your* house? Because if I'm just a guest I'd like my deposit back.

COOPER. You are right and I am wrong and I apologize for that. My house is your house. Do whatever you want. Paint the kitchen. Plant azaleas. Keep a shotgun in the china cabinet if it suits you.

BENNETT. Nope, handgun in the nightstand is sufficient. We should paint this room.

COOPER. Why, what's wrong with this room?

BENNETT. Nothing. But if I can't change the world, I'd like to change this room. Something soothing. Blue.

COOPER. Like a robin's egg blue?

BENNETT. I don't know what that color is, but it sounds lovely. Robin's egg blue please.

COOPER. I'll pick up paint tonight. We can do it this weekend.

BENNETT. I can start tomorrow if I'm out of a job.

COOPER. Do you think you're fired?

BENNETT. Would you fire me if you were her?

COOPER. Oh, God yes. You yelled at that nice lesbian from the TV.

BENNETT. But I was right. And fuck Adam for taking her side. Because I...was *right*.

COOPER. That's why I'd fire you.

BENNETT. Well, shit.

COOPER. Yaaaay, that means you can paint the living room.
BENNETT & COOPER. Yaaaay.

(Lights fade.)

Scene Six

*(The media wall comes to life. **PRESTON**, at her news desk.)*

PRESTON. A thirty-three-year-old man has been placed in a medically-induced coma following an assault early this morning. Atlanta police are still seeking a suspect in the attack on Samuel Garrison, an associate of State Senator Allison Haines. Haines's opponent, Peggy Musgrove, addressed the attack earlier today.

*(**MUSGROVE** stands in front of a hospital logo. Beside her, a middle-aged man and woman, simply dressed. They look tired. The woman holds a framed photo of Sammy in high school, sweet-faced and happy.)*

MUSGROVE. Last night a member of our community, Samuel Garrison, a young man in the prime of his life, was the victim of a vicious attack. It's likely you're going to hear a lot about Samuel, how he came to our city with dreams of being a chef, how he was seduced by a lifestyle that took him away from his dreams. God does not want us to judge Samuel. This young man is someone's child. Paul and Maggie Garrison are here, praying for their son to be restored to health. So I ask you to put politics and judgment aside, and pray for the Garrison family. As parents ourselves, my husband and I can only imagine what they must be experiencing, and we hope that covering the cost of Paul and Maggie's hotel room will provide a small measure of comfort in this tragic time.

*(Back to **PRESTON**.)*

PRESTON. In a written statement, Senator Haines's office offered thoughts and prayers to Garrison's friends and family.

*(The media wall goes dark. **ADAM**, **KIMBERLY**, and **HAINES** stand in the office, gobsmacked.)*

HAINES. Thoughts and prayers? *Thoughts and prayers?!*

KIMBERLY. Bennett wasn't here. I'm not a speechwriter.

HAINES. *Clearly!* And why the hell is Deirdre Preston just giving her free airtime? She might as well be wearing a Musgrove t-shirt.

ADAM. Musgrove gave a better story. She did everything we didn't. Personalized it, made it political while claiming it has nothing to do with politics. She spends two hundred bucks on a room at the DoubleTree and looks like a hero. And we're the assholes who wouldn't address him by name.

HAINES. If I'd done the exact same thing, people would say I'm just feeding my cause. But when Musgrove does it, she comes off as magnanimous. It's a no-win situation. Kimberly, get Bennett on the phone.

KIMBERLY. Are we sure Bennett still works here?

HAINES. If he can get me the upper-hand on Musgrove, then he still works here. I'll say whatever he wants.

ADAM. I think he needs a personal day.

HAINES. Jesus, people, I'm sitting here with egg on my face. I'm trying to make this right. Kimberly, get him on the phone!

*(**KIMBERLY** exits. **ADAM** wavers.)*

Adam. I have to get ready for the Chamber of Commerce gala, and I'm running on about four hours of sleep. So if something's on your mind, quit hovering and just say it.

ADAM. I don't think you're cynical, and I don't think you've fallen completely into the political trap.

HAINES. Thank you. It's reassuring to have my Chief of Staff damn me with such faint praise.

ADAM. But it is worth noting that your response to Sammy's attack was quite different from what you would have said three years ago.

HAINES. Three years ago, I was an activist, I had the luxury of a candid response. Now I'm a politician. Trying desperately to hang on to a job that chips away at everything I hold dear, forces me to wear god-forsaken high heels, and pays me seventeen grand a year for the privilege. There's no place for candor in that scenario. Still wanna run for office one day?

ADAM. Yeah. I do. When the timing's right.

HAINES. Well then, prepare to learn the art of compromise.

    (Lights fade.)

Scene Seven

(A parking lot at twilight. **COOPER** *walks on, holding a gallon of paint. He's on his phone, looking off in the distance, hyperalert and impatient.)*

BENNETT. *(Voice-over.)* Hi, you've reached the personal voicemail of Bennett Riggs. I'm unavailable to take your call right now, but feel free to leave me a message and I'll get back to you at the earliest opportunity. Thank you for calling, and have a great day.

(Beep.)

COOPER. Bennett! Your outgoing message is ridiculous! Answer your goddamn phone! Listen, I'm in the parking lot of Hammond Hardware, and I swear to god, I'm looking at him. I'm looking at Dad Jeans right now. It's him. Fuck me, it's him. He's standing at the MARTA stop, and I don't have that stupid – the card, the business card the detective gave us. Should I call nine-one-one? If he gets on a bus, we're never gonna – I need you to tell me what to do. Bennett. If you're ignoring my call to listen to a fucking podcast, I will set you on fire. I don't know what to do here.

*(***COOPER*** hangs up, continuing to watch.)*

Scene Eight

(The ladies' room at a hotel. **KIMBERLY** *enters, speaking on her cell phone.)*

KIMBERLY. There, can you hear me? Look, babe, Allison hasn't even started her speech, and she still wants to have a meeting at her place after. I don't know, couple of hours. Yes, please, all the food at her house is good for you, I can't handle it. Just pepperoni, I guess. Thin crust.

> *(***MUSGROVE*** *enters, wearing a suit. There is a substantial wine stain on her jacket. She goes to the counter and removes the jacket, revealing a camisole underneath. She tries to repair the damage with a baby wipe from her purse.)*

KIMBERLY. I, um, I gotta go, babe.

> *(***KIMBERLY*** *hangs up and heads for the door.)*

MUSGROVE. You don't know any tricks for this, do you? Look, I know who you work for, I'm just asking if you have any possible solves for a red wine stain.

KIMBERLY. I do not. I have no possible solves.

MUSGROVE. Of course. Fiddlesticks.

KIMBERLY. Fiddlesticks. I think I heard salt, maybe? Sorry. I'm better with kid-related stains.

MUSGROVE. So am I. Well. I suppose I'll have to go home, won't I? Perfect. This is absolutely perfect.

> *(***KIMBERLY*** *digs in her purse, produces a laundry pen.)*

KIMBERLY. Here. Try this.

MUSGROVE. Thank you. Peggy.

KIMBERLY. Oh, I know. Kimberly Phillips. Senator Haines's office manager. And keeper of her laundry pen.

MUSGROVE. I won't tell.

KIMBERLY. If she were in here, she would've offered. Which is the only reason I did.

MUSGROVE. Well. Thanks all the same.

KIMBERLY. Why did you get a hotel room for Sammy Garrison's parents?

MUSGROVE. Oh. Okay. We're talking about that. I got them a hotel room because they needed one.

KIMBERLY. So, just purely for altruistic reasons, you decided to step in?

MUSGROVE. It was the decent thing to do. No one else was helping. Why's that, exactly?

(*She blots for a moment.*)

You're looking for an admission that it was motivated by politics. Alrighty. Moderate voters need to see that I'm not some wild-eyed Bible-beater. But I'm told doing so will also *cost* me votes. From the zealots who spend all day every day thinking about how gay people are destroying America.

KIMBERLY. I thought those people were your base.

MUSGROVE. Cute. That *base* turned out in the primary for three old white men who split the vote. Now I've got to convince them to show up for a black woman. The RNC is pouring money on me because they desperately need my face on TV, but that won't help me win over a bunch of Confederate flag fetishists here at home.

KIMBERLY. But doesn't the fact that you're courting those votes tell you something is really wrong here?

MUSGROVE. Of course it does. But if I don't use my voice, other people are going to speak for me. And lately, I don't like what they're saying. So I put myself forward. That's how things change. My faith teaches me to lead by example. I don't hate anyone. I have my moral standards, but I don't judge and I don't hate.

KIMBERLY. You accepted the endorsement of Reverend Lucas Orton.

MUSGROVE. I did. And his congregation of six thousand.

KIMBERLY. He's pushing for a bathroom bill, Peggy. Do you support it?

MUSGROVE. If elected, I'll address that concern when the people of my district –

KIMBERLY. Don't do that, I've seen your interviews, you're a very artful dodger.

MUSGROVE. That's certainly not my intention.

KIMBERLY. I live in your district. I'm your neighbor. And even though you might not acknowledge it, you've got trans people in your district. They'd be your constituents too. So I'm asking, on behalf of your neighbors, if you support restricting their access to public bathrooms.

MUSGROVE. You're taking a very complicated issue and reducing it to –

KIMBERLY. Because I don't have my birth certificate on me right now. Do you need me to drop my panties and show you the goods? But just seeing my vajeen isn't gonna be enough, is it? They've gotten really good at constructing those things. So you don't know *how long I've had it.*

MUSGROVE. Are you done?

KIMBERLY. Yeah, those were my best lines.

MUSGROVE. Good. Listen. I don't know enough. About this. I know we're not supposed to say things like that because admitting you have more to learn is some sign of weakness, but I haven't sat down with the people who have different viewpoints and listened to them. Compelled a conversation between them. And I will not claim to have a solution to a problem until I've done my homework. Can you appreciate that?

KIMBERLY. I can.

MUSGROVE. Also, my family taught me more than a little about what it feels like to be told which bathrooms you're allowed to use, so rest assured I would tread very carefully on this issue.

(**KIMBERLY** *considers this. She removes her jacket.*)

KIMBERLY. Here. Take it. Get your picture made.

MUSGROVE. Oh, no, I couldn't.

KIMBERLY. You won't get liberal on you, just take the damn thing.

MUSGROVE. Why?

KIMBERLY. Because it's the decent thing to do. And I will not give you the satisfaction of saying I didn't offer. Drop it off at the senator's office sometime.

(**MUSGROVE** *takes the jacket. Puts it on.*)

MUSGROVE. Thank you, Kimberly. Really.

KIMBERLY. Give our best to Sammy's parents. They're in our prayers.

MUSGROVE. Oh, good. I always say prayers from heathens are more effective because God's so surprised to hear from you. Oh, come on, that was funny.

KIMBERLY. Fine. That was funny.

(*Lights fade.*)

Scene Nine

> (**BENNETT**, *in a t-shirt and gym shorts, is applying painter's tape at the kitchen counter while listening to a podcast* on his phone. Doorbell. He pauses the podcast, looks out the peephole, sighs, and opens, revealing* **ADAM** *holding a small pastry box.)*

ADAM. You still have a job.

BENNETT. I shouldn't.

ADAM. But you do. May I come in?

BENNETT. Yeah.

ADAM. Haines says each staff member is allowed to have a meltdown once. It's a freebie. I wish I'd known. I would have used mine by now.

BENNETT. I didn't have a fucking meltdown, Adam. I meant every word I said, and her trivializing it is a little patronizing.

ADAM. She trusts you. She'll listen to you. Come back to work. Or at least come to her place tonight for a conversation.

BENNETT. Allison compromises at every turn just to keep her job. She wouldn't protest at the airports because of the optics. Wouldn't do the march because it was divisive. She used to talk about things that matter.

ADAM. Yes, and look what it got her. She spent her first six months talking about Planned Parenthood, about adoption rights, and now they're using every one of those statements against her, saying she doesn't care about her district. It's a zero-sum game.

BENNETT. You ever think politics are just the theatre we distract ourselves with while other people are out making real change?

---

*A license to produce *Angry Fags* does not include a performance license for any third-party or copyrighted content. Licensees should create an original podcast or use one in the public domain.

ADAM. No, I've never thought that. And I don't believe that's what you really think.

BENNETT. If she gets tired of waiting she can let me go, but I'm not gonna give an answer today.

ADAM. *(Opens the box.)* Here. Some chick in Senator Keating's office had a birthday. There were tiny cupcakes. I stole you a few. They've got booze in 'em.

BENNETT. If I receive the gift of your tiny cupcakes, I want to be clear that it should not be construed as acquiescence to any other offer you've come here to pitch, either professionally or personally.

ADAM. Then you can only have one.

BENNETT. Three. Cut me a break, I'm going through hell and I'm quitting smoking.

ADAM. Two, then.

BENNETT. I accept your terms.

> *(**BENNETT** pops a mini cupcake in his mouth.)*

ADAM. I know you don't think Allison's on your side – on our side – but she is. She's fighting for her political life against that deaf-baby-wielding GOP wet dream, and there have to be certain sacrifices... You okay?

BENNETT. Mm-hm.

ADAM. Something wrong with your cupcake?

BENNETT. *(Shakes his head.)* Mm-mm.

> *(**ADAM** studies him for a moment.)*

ADAM. You forgot to take the wrapper off, didn't you?

BENNETT. *(Shakes his head.)* Mm-mm.

ADAM. You don't want to spit it out, because you're trying not to be gross. You're going to eat that paper.

> *(**BENNETT** grows more determined in chewing.)*

Tell you what. I'm just gonna...look over there. At something. Not over here. So if anything happens over here, I will miss that thing happening.

> *(**ADAM** looks away. **BENNETT** spits something into his napkin. **ADAM** looks back.)*

ADAM. Good cupcake?

BENNETT. Scrumptious.

ADAM. You like me.

BENNETT. Nope.

ADAM. If we were just two coworkers hanging out at your house, you would have spit that cupcake wrapper out right in front of me. But you were willing to actually eat non-food, just for the sake of remaining appealing. Because you like me.

BENNETT. You're saying I must be interested because I'm not willing to regurgitate in front of you?

ADAM. That's the theory I'm floating, yes.

BENNETT. Well. You are wrong. Regurgitating is how I show affection. So I must not like you at all.

ADAM. Were you raised by birds?

BENNETT. Yep.

ADAM. What kind?

BENNETT. Pigeons.

ADAM. Never knew that.

BENNETT. I have many secrets.

ADAM. I'd love to meet your family.

BENNETT. Take french fries to a public park and you will.

ADAM. Glad you don't come from ravens.

BENNETT. Got an issue with ravens?

ADAM. Can't stand 'em.

BENNETT. Are you setting up an Edgar Allen Poe joke?

ADAM. Ravens eat pistachios. Ergo, I can't stand ravens.

BENNETT. Got a thing for pistachios.

ADAM. Grew up on a pistachio farm.

BENNETT. How did I not know this?

ADAM. I have many secrets too.

BENNETT. I don't believe you. It's too randomly specific to possibly be true.

ADAM. Hornsby Farms in Terra Bella, California. Google it. My dad was the ranch manager.

BENNETT. Fascinating. What was that like?

ADAM. Quiet. They didn't switch to machine picking until the late nineties, when I was growing up it was all done by hand. And the seasonal workers didn't come in until harvest time, so most of the year it was just us and a few other families on-site. My mom home-schooled us. We didn't have a TV.

BENNETT. That's not normal.

ADAM. I'm aware of that. My family was pretty –

BENNETT. Nuts?

ADAM. I was going to say insular.

BENNETT. See what I did there?

ADAM. I see what you did there.

BENNETT. You didn't have a TV?

ADAM. Nope. I have some pretty serious gaps in my pop culture knowledge base.

BENNETT. *That's* why you don't know who Julia Sugarbaker is. I just thought you were trying for a straight-acting thing. Holy shit, you missed all eighties television. *Designing Women. Quantum Leap.* The fucking *Golden Girls*. Do you even know who Alf is?

ADAM. No idea what you're talking about.

BENNETT. Jesus. You've missed so much. Do you at least watch TV now?

ADAM. I freakin' love TV. TV is the reason I got in to politics. I discovered *The West Wing* my freshman year of college, because my roommate loved it, and by season three I'd switched to Poli Sci. One day I wanna be just like Jed Bartlet, only super gay.

BENNETT. Well of course you do. It was the first TV show you'd ever seen, you were so impressionable. If your roommate had loved *Murphy Brown*, you'd wanna be a famous reporter with a bastard baby.

ADAM. You lost me again.

BENNETT. Damn it, I'm saying funny shit here, and you don't get my references. You just got dropped into our terrifying modern world. It's like you're on Rumspringa.

(No reaction.)

BENNETT. Oh, for Chrissakes, you're so sheltered you don't even get Amish jokes!

ADAM. Okay, we've covered me. Now let's make fun of your personal history. What do your parents do?

BENNETT. Argue. They're divorced. My father works in demolition. Not construction. Just demolition. What sort of person, do you think, would be drawn to a career where all he does is destroy things?

ADAM. And your mom?

BENNETT. Moved to Maine with her new husband. She had twins at forty-two. It was disgusting. Anyway, she got a do-over, and I got a little lost in the shuffle.

ADAM. Well, lucky for you, kids are resilient. Even the messed-up parents can still accidentally turn out a good one. Look at me. The progeny of reclusive nut harvesters, and I'm a freakin' catch.

BENNETT. You don't know who Alf is. You have flaws.

ADAM. Who is this Alf person, and why is he so important?

BENNETT. He's this kinda anteater-inspired space alien who talks like an old Jew and eats housecats.

ADAM. You're lying. This is like the pigeon thing.

BENNETT. He had his own sitcom! Might be on Hulu. It's tantamount to child abuse, depriving a child of Alf and rearing them in a nut-plucking nightmare.

ADAM. It wasn't a nightmare. It was all I knew.

BENNETT. But now you know better.

ADAM. In a way, I guess. But it was also kinda amazing. After dinner on warm nights, I'd just lie in the hammock, look up at the stars. For hours. Picture any kid you know being still, and silent, *for hours*.

BENNETT. I would like that kid.

ADAM. And when pistachios are ripe for harvest, the shell pops open. It's this little *shhhp* sound, if it was only one you wouldn't notice it, but it starts a chain reaction, so it's thousands of these tiny sounds, all around you.

(He demonstrates.)

And that sound meant that tomorrow there'd be dozens of people coming in, and they'd make me tamales wrapped up in newspaper, and we'd sing and tell stories... I'd lie out there for weeks, every year, waiting for that first little *shhhp* sound. I thought it was the most exciting thing in the whole world. My crazy parents gave me that.

BENNETT. Do the sound again.

*(He does. **BENNETT** kisses him.)*

I like that.

ADAM. Me too.

BENNETT. Do it again.

*(**ADAM** makes the sound. A kiss. A good one.)*

You wanna see my room?

ADAM. Yes I do.

*(They rise, **ADAM** tugging at **BENNETT**'s shorts, **BENNETT** unbuttoning **ADAM**'s shirt. It's all very fumbly and awkward and fun. **BENNETT** runs down the hall. **ADAM** follows. Lights fade.)*

Scene Ten

(The hotel ladies' room. **HAINES,** *in an evening gown, enters, going to the mirror and blotting her makeup.* **PRESTON** *enters, also dressed for a formal event.)*

PRESTON. A meeting in the ladies' room. Takes me back to high school.

HAINES. Back then I didn't have an assistant to guard the door.

PRESTON. Really? I did.

HAINES. I'm sorry, Deirdre, I thought I'd have more time but they want me back out there for the step-and-repeat.

PRESTON. You've got time. There was quite a line for photos with Peggy Musgrove.

HAINES. I'm sure. Are you covering this event or just attending?

PRESTON. If I'm showing cleavage it means I'm off the clock.

HAINES. Well then keep your tits out, because we need to talk off the record.

PRESTON. Happy to oblige.

HAINES. Every time you mention my office in the same breath as Sammy Garrison's assault, it implies a connection which does not exist.

PRESTON. We don't know that to be true. The suspect is still at-large.

HAINES. Sammy was a volunteer. My speechwriter's ex-boyfriend. This has nothing to do with me.

PRESTON. And if that's the case, the investigation will bear it out. Trust the process, Senator.

HAINES. The process is broken. People trust the narrative, and you're manipulating it.

PRESTON. I'm completely neutral. Just reporting.

HAINES. Oh fuck off, Deirdre, you're manufacturing drama. Trying to surround me with controversy while you're lobbing softballs at Peggy Musgrove.

PRESTON. You need to contour better. You were totally washed-out up there.

(**PRESTON** *produces a contour palette and brush from her purse.*)

May I?

(**HAINES** *submits.*)

I've been at this for a while, and I've learned to spot an...energy. It can suddenly surround a person. They capture the public's imagination, assuage their fears and elevate their hopes. They become the zeitgeist, and they are *annointed*. Obama at the DNC in 2004. Trump, at the second Republican debate. Nothing is guaranteed, of course. I saw it with Ann Richards in eighty-eight, but Ferraro had scorched the earth for at least twelve years. Heather Wilson in 2004, but the Republicans weren't thinking ahead. Peggy Musgrove has that energy. An energy stronger than qualifications, or message, or facts. If I come for her, my viewers will mutiny, and I lose my voice. In trying to get to the truth, I will lose their trust. Ain't that a bitch?

HAINES. I have more faith in people than that.

PRESTON. I know. That's why you're going to lose. As for me? I will be the journalist who treated Peggy Musgrove with respect and fairness. And the people who support her will continue to trust me when she's in the governor's office, or the U.S. Senate, or...who knows?

(*She steps back, her work complete.*)

It's the world we're living in now, Allison. We adapt.

HAINES. When this country returns to reasonable, rational discourse – and we will – people like you are going to have a lot to answer for, Deirdre.

PRESTON. The day you're imagining isn't coming. You're trying to play according to a rulebook which no longer exists. People like you never win the fight because you're too afraid to get your hands dirty.

> (**PRESTON** *exits as we return to Bennett and Cooper's. The front door opens.* **COOPER** *steps in, covered in blue paint and what appears to be blood.)*

COOPER. Bennett! Bennett! Goddamn it, *Bennett*!

BENNETT. *(Offstage.)* Not now!

COOPER. No, now!

BENNETT. *(Offstage.)* Oh for Chrissakes –

> (**BENNETT** *enters in his shorts.)*

What the hell?

COOPER. I tried to call you.

BENNETT. Cooper, what's going on?

COOPER. I had to make a choice.

BENNETT. Cooper, what did you do?

COOPER. I made it better.

> *(Blackout.)*

End of Act One

ACT TWO

Scene Eleven

(**COOPER** *enters in a t-shirt and underwear, checking his phone.* **BENNETT** *is asleep on the sofa. He stirs and rises.*)

BENNETT. Shit, I fell asleep.

COOPER. Yes, while I was taking my Silkwood shower.

BENNETT. You and I didn't finish talking.

COOPER. Aww, I hope we never do. You're my dearest friend and I enjoy our talks. Tell me more about Adam. Are you two an item now?

BENNETT. No.

COOPER. Fucking the boss, I love it. You saucy little minx.

BENNETT. Adam is not my boss, he's my coworker. And we're not having sex.

COOPER. Just a little Princeton rub on the conference table?

BENNETT. No idea what that is.

COOPER. Look it up, you'll love it.

BENNETT. You don't know for a fact that you had the right guy.

COOPER. Actually, I do. Because I looked at him and saw he was the person he was. I refuse to rehash this.

BENNETT. What are the odds of you just running into him?

COOPER. Odds are irrelevant, because I did. There's nothing on any of the news sites about it. Isn't that fitting? No one even misses him.

BENNETT. You're certain he was dead?

COOPER. Do not ask me again.

BENNETT. ...You're sure.

COOPER. I bashed his fucking skull in with a paint can *and* a brick. Then I smothered him with a shopping bag. This is just like when I load the dishwasher. You go back and check my work and it is offensive.

BENNETT. Because as we've learned from the dishwasher, you are occasionally not as thorough as you need to be. You gotta go back to the hardware store this morning, tell them you accidentally left a gallon of paint sitting in the parking lot. It's a custom color. They're going to remember you.

COOPER. That's good, that's solid.

BENNETT. If you answer the question before it's asked, you set the terms.

COOPER. You're such a political animal. I should get involved in politics, you make it all sound so intriguing. God, I just remembered you're unemployed. I'll bet Allison had you blacklisted by the gay mafia.

BENNETT. Adam says I still have a job.

COOPER. Ohhh, *that's* why you let him fuck you! You saucy little minx, nothing like getting job security face down on the mattress, right?

BENNETT. We did not have sex. And why do you assume I'm a bottom?

COOPER. You fit the profile. You do a lot of squats and you take a fiber supplement. Who wants coffee? It'll make you feel normal.

BENNETT. I am normal. I didn't do anything.

COOPER. You're an accessory after the fact.

BENNETT. Only thing that separates us from the animals is our ability to accessorize.

COOPER. You just quoted *Steel Magnolias* while we're discussing me killing a man.

BENNETT. And I am ashamed. Put on some damn clothes.

COOPER. Later. I think the initial shock has passed here, and I would like a little credit. I took evil out of this world last night. Just admit that you're glad I did it. I slayed the dragon. I made it better.

BENNETT. Dammit, there's no Splenda. You cannot seriously be expecting me to thank you.

COOPER. I stood up for the tribe. I got results.

BENNETT. You made a mess. Yes, ultimately I do think justice was served, but it was an irrational move, so much could have gone wrong.

COOPER. But it didn't. You are welcome.

BENNETT. No! No thank you! This was messy and impulsive and you could have been caught. Hell, you *still* could be. And I'll do everything I can to keep that from happening, but you gotta work with me here. You're the one constant I can actually depend on.

COOPER. I know. That's why I did it.

BENNETT. So the next time you have a hankerin' to dispense vigilante justice, promise we'll have a planning session of some kind?

COOPER. Cross my heart.

BENNETT. Good. I think I've got Splenda in my backpack.

(*He exits to the hall.*)

COOPER. Who would you pick? If you had a hankerin' to dispense vigilante justice?

BENNETT. I really don't want to have this conversation.

COOPER. Come on. Who?

BENNETT. (*Returning with packets.*) I don't know. If it's worldwide, maybe Putin? Or head over to Chechnya and take out Kadyrov.

COOPER. No idea who that is.

BENNETT. You really need to follow the news.

COOPER. I'm following the news right this second.

BENNETT. Not just on days when you're seeing if they found the guy you murdered.

COOPER. Not murder! Justifiable homicide. Self-defense.

BENNETT. There's no such thing as self-defense by proxy.

COOPER. Well, if there were, who would you pick?

BENNETT. ...Mark Fredericks. You have no idea who that is either. He's the head of the Faith and Family Foundation. At work we just call them The Big F. Bunch of Brooks Brothers and Buckhead Betty bigots. Mark Fredericks is their toothy overlord – if I had the chance, I would blow him up. Kaboom.

COOPER. You know who I'd get?

BENNETT. Why do you get another one?

COOPER. Dad Jeans was for Sammy. I want one just for me, and I would pick Reverend Lucas Orton.

BENNETT. Well yes, he should die.

COOPER. You remember Jason, used to work at Outwrite Bookstore?

BENNETT. Blonde Jason or Ginger Jason?

COOPER. Ginger Jason. Well, now he works at Aqua – that nasty bathhouse behind Krispy Kreme? He says Reverend Orton is in there *all the time*. Sits in the back of the steam room, creeping for a beej.

BENNETT. Before heading back to the pulpit to condemn us all to hell. Yes. Kill him. Kill him dead.

COOPER. If you had the opportunity, would you? I mean, really. Would you?

BENNETT. If I had the chance? Yeah. I think I would.

COOPER. No you wouldn't.

BENNETT. Don't tell me I wouldn't. I would. I would kill the fuck out of that guy. And I'd keep it clean and simple. Bludgeoning someone in a parking lot is a wee bit operatic for my taste.

COOPER. What's *your* style, darling?

BENNETT. Chloroform. In large amounts it causes cardiac arrest. I'm sure you can buy it online.

COOPER. Why do you know this?

BENNETT. Because you can get anything online.

COOPER. I mean about how chloroform works?

BENNETT. I think I read it in a book. John Grisham, Patricia Cornwell, one of those. I remember thinking, "Oh, that's efficient." No cleanup. Hell, you could take him down in a private room at the bathhouse.

COOPER. People wear nothing but towels there, and you're wandering around with a bottle of chloroform?

BENNETT. You see? I hadn't thought of that. This is why we'd need those planning sessions. I should get dressed. What's better for groveling, stripes or solids?

COOPER. Oh, stripes, no question.

BENNETT. Remember to go by the hardware store. And Coop. Thank you. For making coffee. It means a lot, knowing you'll take care of things.

(*Lights fade as* **BENNETT** *exits.*)

Scene Twelve

(Haines's office. **KIMBERLY** *is putting together media kits.* **ADAM** *enters.)*

ADAM. Morning.

KIMBERLY. I hate you so much, just shut your face.

ADAM. I'm sorry.

KIMBERLY. Okay first, she came out of the bathroom with her face beat like a Kardashian, then she launches into this very complicated tirade about Deirdre Preston making fake news, I'm still trying to wrap my brain around it. And *then* she kept me at her house until almost midnight. "Try Adam again, Kimberly." "Have you tried Bennett?" Oh. Oh! By the fucking way, Madeline has taken up clarinet. She only knows "Hot Cross Buns." So I got to listen to Haines's damn daughter make hot cross buns for ninety goddamn minutes. It sounded like a goose having the longest orgasm ever recorded.

ADAM. I'm sorry.

KIMBERLY. Where were you? Why were you ignoring my calls? Because if it's for any reason other than you two having sex, I will not accept it.

ADAM. ...

KIMBERLY. Holy shit! Finally! Okay, I'll tell you how I picture it, and you tell me what I get right.

ADAM. No. That's odd.

KIMBERLY. "Hot Cross Buns," you bastard! Let me have this!

ADAM. Okay, well, I knew he was interested because he almost ate paper – it was cute, just trust me. Then we talked about pigeons, he explained who Alf is. Then I gave an overview of nut farming that made him tear my clothes off.

KIMBERLY. So far we're pretty removed from what I pictured.

ADAM. We got to the bedroom –

KIMBERLY. Yeah.

ADAM. And for a while we just, you know, kissed and talked –

KIMBERLY. Sweet, boring, keep going –

ADAM. And then clothes start coming off, and he leaves the room –

KIMBERLY. To get condoms! No, lube! What, like whipped cream! Tell me when to stop!

ADAM. Please stop. He comes back in…I'm naked…and he says…his roommate is in crisis and I need to leave. So I put on my clothes and went home. The end.

KIMBERLY. Why do you people not know how to be gay? Don't you watch Logo?

ADAM. I'm gonna need you to stop watching Logo. The people on that network are basically sociopaths.

KIMBERLY. Did you at least get him to come back to work?

ADAM. I have no idea what he's going to do.

KIMBERLY. You failed on every level, do you know that?

ADAM. Yes, I know that.

KIMBERLY. Now, as penance, please type up the story about nut farming that makes people tear your clothes off, because I intend to put that to use.

      (**BENNETT** *enters, dressed for work.*)

BENNETT. Good morning.

ADAM. Good morning.

KIMBERLY. …What's up?

BENNETT. Oh, you know, the usual.

      (**BENNETT** *sits. Opens his laptop. Begins working.* **KIMBERLY** *and* **ADAM** *watch this with great interest.* **HAINES** *enters, engrossed in her phone. She walks past* **BENNETT**. *Then stops.*)

HAINES. Bennett.

BENNETT. Senator.

HAINES. Did you see the numbers in the AJC this morning?

BENNETT. Musgrove had a momentary bounce from the press conference with Sammy's parents. It'll settle.

HAINES. Do we have a statement?

BENNETT. We do.

HAINES. Is it fucking brilliant?

BENNETT. Pretty close.

HAINES. Good to have you back. We fall apart without you. We lost you for one day and Kimberly played dress-up with Peggy Musgrove.

(**HAINES** *exits.*)

KIMBERLY. It was a jacket. I was trying to – oh, for fuck's sake you had to be there. I'm getting coffee.

(**KIMBERLY** *exits.*)

BENNETT. I owe you an apology.

ADAM. No, you don't.

BENNETT. But I do. Cooper had a freakout, it's too stupid to even go into.

ADAM. Everything okay? He sounded like he was in a panic when he came home.

BENNETT. Oh, no, he was home the whole time. He was just holed up in his room until he decided to rope me into his meltdown, it's nothing new, already over.

ADAM. Oh. Good.

BENNETT. However. There is the pressing problem of – I got to see you naked, but only for like five seconds. *And* I don't think it's fair that I've seen you naked and you haven't seen me naked.

ADAM. I am also struck by the unfairness of that.

BENNETT. Wanna see me naked?

ADAM. Right now?

BENNETT. No, the lighting in here's terrible. After work.

ADAM. So when you get naked later, are you thinking I'll be naked too?

BENNETT. Entirely up to you. But my preference is that both of us are naked. At the same time. And doin' stuff.

ADAM. This is the hottest awkward conversation I've ever had.

(**BENNETT** *grabs him. A kiss.* **KIMBERLY** *returns with coffee.*)

KIMBERLY. Now grab his ass.

ADAM. We are not your porn!

KIMBERLY. Yes, it's best if you think that. Hey, did y'all hear about the dead guy they found in Midtown, made up to look like one of the Blue Man Group? It is a sick world, boys.

> *(Lights fade.)*

Scene Thirteen

(The media wall comes to life. **PRESTON** *interviewing* **REVEREND LUCAS ORTON.***)*

PRESTON. Reverend Lucas Orton, you're the pastor of a church with over six thousand members, most of them families. Wouldn't people reasonably expect you to support an anti-bullying initiative?

ORTON. See, that's the clever mischaracterization of this initiative, which is really just another subversive effort on behalf of the liberal agenda. What these activists really want to do is take away free speech and annihilate a healthy learning environment.

PRESTON. So, when you hear statements like, "No child should ever feel hungry, stalked, frightened, terrorized, bullied, isolated or afraid, with nowhere to turn," would you say you disagree with that?

ORTON. I would say that it's a smokescreen, Deirdre. Designed to obfuscate their true intentions.

PRESTON. Reverend Orton, that quote is from Melania Trump.

ORTON. And I absolutely agree with Mrs. Trump that when anyone with good Christian morals tries to set these misguided young people on a righteous path, these deviant predators, like Senator Allison Haines, an unrepentant female Sodomite, will swoop in –

PRESTON. I'm sorry, Reverend Orton, at what point did Mrs. Trump say any of these things?

ORTON. Mrs. Trump understands our children are under attack, and so do I.

> *(The media wall goes dark. The common area in a bathhouse.* **BENNETT** *enters, wearing a tiny white towel, which he keeps trying to make larger through stretching, fidgeting, and what appears to be prayer. He leans against a wall and scans the room.* **COOPER** *enters, also in a towel.)*

COOPER. You beat me here.

BENNETT. Isn't it weird? I always pictured this place as, you know, Sodom with a pool. But it just feels like the locker room at the Y.

(They scan the room. **COOPER** *sits.)*

These things are the size of a Kleenex. Why do they even bother giving you a towel?

COOPER. Mine fits.

BENNETT. Well, I have an ass.

COOPER. Stop fidgeting. You're drawing attention to yourself.

BENNETT. My midsection looks better when I'm standing.

COOPER. You look like a prairie dog. Sit.

*(***BENNETT*** *sits.)*

BENNETT. Where is it?

COOPER. You'll love this. I'm a mastermind. I'm wearing a cock sock.

BENNETT. A what?

COOPER. You know, like actors wear in nude scenes so you can't see their junk?

BENNETT. I did not know that was a thing.

COOPER. It's a thing. Very breathable, I rather like it. And you know what's inside the cock sock?

BENNETT. Your penis.

COOPER. My penis. Also, a small steel cylinder. Inside the cylinder? Chloroform.

BENNETT. You have a vial of chloroform next to your dick? That sounds like a horrible idea.

COOPER. It's made of steel, I'm totally secure.

BENNETT. Ginger Jason said he's still here?

COOPER. Yep.

BENNETT. Did he ask why we wanted to know?

COOPER. I told him we wanted to get video of Reverend Orton to sell to TMZ.

BENNETT. Coop. Over there. Looking right at us.

COOPER. Oh God, he looks like a constipated walrus.

BENNETT. Coo-coo-ca-choo.

(They erupt into giggles.)

COOPER. Fuck me, this is insane. Are we doing this? We are not doing this. This is the stupidest thing I've ever done. And I wore YMLA metallic muscle shirts for like two years.

BENNETT. But we had a planning session.

COOPER. We don't have to go through with it just because you made a PowerPoint.

BENNETT. You need me to do the warmup?

COOPER. Do the warmup.

BENNETT. Reverend Orton's primary goal and singular preoccupation is the denial of our civil rights. He is a proven force of evil in this world. As long as he has breath in his body, he will fight to destroy us. Nothing gets better unless we make it better. We will protect the tribe. Make it better, Coop.

COOPER. Right.

BENNETT. Right.

COOPER. Fuck yes. Brilliant.

BENNETT. You good?

COOPER. Yes, okay. Yes. Okay, fuck it, let's do this. If anyone comes toward the room, get them away from there, I don't care if you have to blow 'em to do it.

BENNETT. Let's save that as a last resort.

COOPER. You've done a lot more for a lot less.

> *(**COOPER** rises and struts off. **BENNETT** tries to casually observe while still fidgeting with his towel. Moments pass. And **COOPER** is back.)*

I just got rejected by a constipated walrus.

BENNETT. Oh, honey. We did not plan for that.

COOPER. Why would we? I never plan for rejection.

BENNETT. So... Mission aborted?

COOPER. No, but there's a change in the lineup. He *was* looking over here. Just not at me.

BENNETT. Oh. No. Oh no sir. I'll have to make out with him or give him a handie to get close enough, and I can't do that because I'm kind of seeing someone.

COOPER. Yes, wouldn't want you to have any secrets from Adam, you've been on three whole dates. I'm going swimming.

BENNETT. No no no. We may not get this chance again.

COOPER. I know that. But there's nothing I can do, he's just not that into me.

BENNETT. Okay, okay. Sorry.

COOPER. Smile at the walrus.

> (**BENNETT** *gives a pained smile.*)

Protect the tribe.

BENNETT. Protect the tribe. Make it better.

COOPER. Make it better.

> (*He reaches under his towel.*)

Act like you're jacking off. I'm gonna pass you the cock sock.

> (**BENNETT** *reaches under his towel and simulates activity.* **COOPER** *discreetly passes him a flesh-colored pouch, which* **BENNETT** *slips under the towel.*)

BENNETT. How does this thing work?

COOPER. It snaps underneath, just like a cock ring.

BENNETT. I've never worn a cock ring.

COOPER. Well, look at all the new experiences you're having. Will you stop making that face?

BENNETT. I have no idea what I'm doing, and there are volatile chemicals next to my dick, you dick.

COOPER. Oh, for shit's sake. Stand up and face me.

> (**BENNETT** *does.* **COOPER** *gets on his knees.*)

COOPER. Put your hands on your hips, look at him, and act like I'm fluffing you.

>*(***BENNETT*** *attempts to put his hands on his hips while opening his towel modestly.* ***COOPER*** *loses patience and tugs it off of him, dropping it to the floor.* ***COOPER*** *stares at* ***BENNETT****'s crotch.)*

BENNETT. What's wrong?

COOPER. When did you start sleeping with Adam?

BENNETT. What?

COOPER. You're freshly manscaped, Bennett. Nobody mows the yard unless company's coming over.

BENNETT. Can we please have this conversation when my cock is not in your face?

>*(***COOPER*** *secures the pouch.* ***BENNETT*** *looks over his shoulder and attempts a come-hither face.* ***COOPER*** *hands* ***BENNETT*** *the towel, which he secures around his waist once more.)*

COOPER. Fine.

BENNETT. My stomach hurts.

COOPER. Do not throw up on him.

BENNETT. He's a proven force of evil in this world.

COOPER. He'll only get more powerful with time. And there's only one person in the world who can stop him.

BENNETT. I'm gonna stop him.

BENNETT & COOPER. Protect the tribe.

COOPER. Here's your one chance, Fancy. Don't let me down.

>*(***BENNETT*** *walks off.* ***COOPER*** *watches like a proud parent as lights fade.)*

Scene Fourteen

(Haines's office. Night. **HAINES** *is at her desk, working, a box from Savage Pizza nearby.* **MUSGROVE** *enters, holding Kimberly's jacket in a dry-cleaner bag.)*

MUSGROVE. Senator?

HAINES. Mrs. Musgrove. This is a surprise.

MUSGROVE. Peggy, please.

HAINES. Allison.

MUSGROVE. Alright. I was in the building, I had a meeting... I don't suppose your office manager is still here.

HAINES. Kimberly's gone for the day. Is that her jacket?

MUSGROVE. Oh. Yes. I had it cleaned. There's a note in the pocket. She really saved me that night.

HAINES. *(Extending her hand)* I'm glad.

(A handshake. Awkward.)

Sit, please.

MUSGROVE. I can only stay for a moment. It's already so late, and I'm starving.

HAINES. Public service. The hours are terrible. I've got a couple slices left if you'd like one.

MUSGROVE. Actually? That'd be wonderful.

*(***HAINES*** *retrieves the pizza box.)*

HAINES. How you holding up?

MUSGROVE. It's certainly been a lifestyle change. I haven't seen my kids awake in days.

HAINES. How old are they?

MUSGROVE. Nine, six, and Bailey's seven months.

HAINES. Make breakfast sacrosanct. Drag 'em outta bed a half hour earlier if you need to. They'll fight you on it, but it's better if they see your face every morning.

MUSGROVE. I'll keep that in mind.

HAINES. It's the effective routine we found after a lot of failures. Have you been in touch with Sammy Garrison's parents?

MUSGROVE. Today, actually. Maggie says they don't expect him to wake up. His kidneys are failing.

HAINES. I can't imagine what they're going through.

MUSGROVE. They asked my opinion, I told them they should let him be at peace.

HAINES. That is...unexpected.

MUSGROVE. I lost my father to colon cancer three years ago. It is horrifying, how long it can take for our bodies to go, you know? If they can be spared that hell, it'd be a blessing. Paul and Maggie are letting his friends come in to say their goodbyes, so if you'll convey that to – to your staff –

HAINES. I will. That's very kind of you, Peggy.

MUSGROVE. I'm sure you think I'm an awful person. I'm not.

HAINES. I don't think you are. I am very impressed by you. If circumstances were different, we'd probably work very well together. I don't suppose you'd consider moving to another district, running again?

MUSGROVE. No, but you're more than welcome to.

HAINES. Right after I was elected, the speaker of the house turned eighty. I wanted to do something special for him, to show we can all celebrate together, you know? I gave him a bottle of Penfolds Shiraz. It's a three hundred dollar bottle of wine.

MUSGROVE. Wow. Okay.

HAINES. Yeah, my wife's a lawyer. And we're wine snobs. So. I saw the speaker in the hall a few weeks later, asked if he'd tried the wine, he said yes. They'd made sangria out of it. He took that Shiraz and mixed it with 7Up and bananas. Peggy, you are a three hundred dollar bottle of wine. And if you're elected, they're gonna try to make shitty sangria out of you.

MUSGROVE. Allison, you've been blocked on every piece of legislation you've introduced for the last two years.

They're not going to work with you. I can change from within. You can't. And it's not because you're a liberal, or because you're gay. It's because you can't accept the idea that some people like sangria. You're the sort of person who gives someone a gift and also wants to control how they use it.

HAINES. I think you're missing the point.

MUSGROVE. No, I think *you* are. I've voted for plenty of Democrats. If that spot on the ballot had been available I could've swung that way. I'm running as a Republican because that was where the opportunity was, and I want to win. I'll do more good for our district working from inside the belly of the beast than you ever could howling at the wind on the outside.

HAINES. They are using you, Peggy. To the national committee, the press, you're a curiosity. But the very first time you go against party lines, they'll start making plans to primary you out. You'll be a one-term wonder. A footnote. And you'll have taken the opportunity to do real work away from both of us.

> (**MUSGROVE***'s phone rings, followed almost immediately by* **HAINES***'s landline and cell phone.*)

Whoa.

> (*Each answers their phone.*)

MUSGROVE.	**HAINES.**
Go ahead.	Allison Haines.

HAINES. What?

MUSGROVE. Oh my word.

> (*To* **HAINES.**)

Do you have cable in here?

> (**HAINES** *grabs a remote and the media wall comes to life. It's* **PRESTON**, *at her desk.*)

PRESTON. Reverend Orton was found in a private guest room by one of the facility attendants, dead of an apparent heart attack. Witnesses report that Orton had spent several hours in the facility's steam room and sauna areas, which could have raised his blood pressure to dangerous levels. Sources indicate Reverend Orton was a frequent patron at Aqua, a bathhouse catering to gay male clientele, whose website offers quote, "nude sunbathing, a steam room maze, and a sensual, inviting grotto," end quote. Reverend Lucas Orton achieved national prominence as the pastor of –

(**HAINES** *turns off the television.*)

MUSGROVE. That son of a bitch. He endorsed me two weeks ago.

HAINES. But you must have known this could happen.

MUSGROVE. Why would I have known that?

HAINES. Peggy. Everybody knew about Lucas Orton. He was an open secret to everyone but Mrs. Orton.

MUSGROVE. He wasn't to me! Nobody told me!

HAINES. Well, that's just funny, I'm sorry. You want a list of closeted hypocrites in Georgia politics?

MUSGROVE. Yes! I would very much like that list!

HAINES. You know, Peggy, there's a possibility here. You have the ear of his demographic, you could speak to the sad fact that Lucas Orton felt he couldn't live honestly, try to promote some kind of understanding. Hell, we could make a statement together. Promote compassion –

MUSGROVE. It would promote nothing but your agenda. Isn't it enough that you've spent the last two years abusing this office for your personal cause? God, the ego on you.

HAINES. Peggy, that's not it at all –

MUSGROVE. Lucas Orton was a manipulative coward, and a liar. If you want to take pity on him, you go right ahead. But this election is about the issues affecting District Fifty-Seven. At some point you might want to find out what those are. Thank you for the pizza. Good night.

(**MUSGROVE** *departs. Lights fade.*)

Scene Fifteen

(A few days later. The media wall shows the closing credits of a television show as music plays. **BENNETT** *and* **ADAM** *tangled on the sofa.* **BENNETT** *has a notebook and pen.* **ADAM** *hits the remote, the wall goes dark.)*

BENNETT. Verdict?

ADAM. That was really good TV. *Quantum Leap* is absolutely in the "Yes" column.

BENNETT. That makes no damn sense. Yes to *Quantum Leap*, but no to *Sliders*? They're basically the same premise. And *Sliders* has Jerry O'Connell *in his prime*.

ADAM. Mm. I disagree. Nobody's prime is in their twenties. A lot of people *think* their twenties are their prime, but it's just impossible.

BENNETT. And why's that?

ADAM. Because you can't be in your prime when you're still stupid, and everyone's stupid in their twenties.

BENNETT. When do we stop being stupid?

ADAM. Some never do. What, you want like a number here?

BENNETT. I want an exact earliest possible date of non-stupidity.

ADAM. Women, twenty-six. Men, twenty-nine. The looming thirties snap us into focus at the last minute. It's common knowledge. This is why you have to be thirty-five to run for president. So you're a little removed from stupid. Ideally.

BENNETT. Oh, good, so you feel like you're pretty much ready to run?

ADAM. A few more years, then I'll be ready.

　　　　*(***BENNETT** *laughs. Alone.)*

---

*A license to produce *Angry Fags* does not include a performance license for any third-party or copyrighted music. Licensees should create an original composition or use music in the public domain. For further information, please see Music Use Note on page 3.

BENNETT. Dear god you're serious.

ADAM. I told you I wanna be just like Jed Bartlet from *West Wing*, only super gay.

BENNETT. You want to be the first gay president?

ADAM. I don't care if I'm first. Nah, that's a lie, I wanna be first. Why are you looking at me like that? You don't think a gay guy could get elected?

BENNETT. I mean, eventually. Like, generations from now. We couldn't even get a straight woman in. A straight woman who *got the most votes*.

ADAM. Hillary didn't lose because she's a woman. She lost because she's Hillary.

BENNETT. If you say it's because she wasn't likeable you lose access to my dick for three days.

ADAM. Likeable. Fuck likeable. Hillary had one moment when she could've seized her opportunity and rode the wave to the presidency, but she backed off, she compromised. She couldn't do it.

BENNETT. Do what?

ADAM. Leave Bill. If she had left him in 1998, while she was still First Lady, can you imagine? New York still would've elected her, she would've gone into the 2008 race a feminist icon. Probably beat Obama. The greatest second act in American political history. Instead, she compromised. I think she truly loved him, but that's beside the point. All those women? They were telling the truth. Monica, Paula Jones, Gennifer Flowers. We all knew it was true, but she forgave him, so as progressives we had to forgive him too. For the good of the country. And secretly, we hated her for it. For forcing us to let it go, because she did. That was our original sin. It set the standard that allowed a proud pussy-grabber to take the oath of office twenty years later.

BENNETT. I'm sorry, I don't think you mean to sound as misogynistic as you do right now.

ADAM. To the contrary, I'm criticizing her decision *not* to fully own her power. She had to choose. Take a stand, make a sacrifice, and secure the future. Or ignore all the evidence, call every single one of those women liars, and bet on a bad horse. Once the decision was made, her moment passed.

BENNETT. How the hell does someone know when they're facing a moment like that?

ADAM. I'm honestly not sure. I guess when you're faced with a seemingly impossible decision, you know you've reached your moment.

BENNETT. Yeah, that makes sense.

(His phone rings.)

Fuck you, phone.

(He answers.)

Bennett Riggs... Who? Oh. Oh, hi.

*(Lights fade. **ADAM** exits. **BENNETT** does not.)*

Scene Sixteen

*(The sound of a respirator. A single pool of
light.* **BENNETT** *steps in from the darkness.)*

BENNETT. Your mom called me. Finally. I really thought I'd
never see you again. I know I'm not supposed to make
this all about me, but...well, I'm doing all the talking,
so we'll just go with it unless you chime in. I kept
thinking, if it had happened a month earlier, I would
have been with you. Or we would have been home,
and you wouldn't have been at the bar at all. If I had
forgiven you, this wouldn't have happened.

And maybe I was too harsh, ending it all because you
slept with that fucking fetus from your gym. I never
should have let you join a gym. Nothing good happens
there. But I knew it wasn't just him. I was with you for
three years, Sammy, I knew you.

And I still loved you. You were wonderful in so many
ways. Just not that way. I wasn't enough. And I wanted
to be enough for someone.

The man who did this to you is dead. He got his head
bashed in. He suffered. Cooper did it. And you thought
he never liked you.

We're not going to be victims anymore. I killed Reverend
Lucas Orton, you know from TV? In a bathhouse. I
wore a cock sock. Many things have happened. But
when it seems random, it doesn't really say anything,
does it? People won't sit up and pay attention until they
know *why* it's happening. You will not die in vain.

(He pulls out his phone and dials. **COOPER**
*is revealed as his phone rings, sitting at a
folding table piled with envelopes.)*

COOPER. Hey.

BENNETT. I'm here.

COOPER. You okay?

BENNETT. Yeah, I just can't seem to leave. God, I wish I had a cigarette.

COOPER. I can leave right now and bring you a pack. No judgment.

BENNETT. No, it's fine. Tell me something totally superficial.

COOPER. Okie dokie. I met a real-live Log Cabin Republican today. And he's *our age.*

BENNETT. Weird. What's he like?

COOPER. Dunno. I've been steering clear while I sniff him out. His name's David. He's totally wholesome hot, like Fred Savage. But he's said like three complimentary things about Mike Pence. So my penis is very confused.

BENNETT. Wait a minute. Where are you right now?

COOPER. I'm all by myself. *Doing volunteer work.*

BENNETT. You mean –

COOPER. Oh, I mean.

BENNETT. Coop, *no.* How long have you been doing this?

COOPER. Just like a week.

BENNETT. Coop, we did not discuss this.

COOPER. I feel like we did.

BENNETT. We did not.

COOPER. Well I can't leave now, I'm popular here. They call me Thomas. I haven't used my first name since I was in third grade, it's like I'm a parallel universe version of myself, crazy, right?

BENNETT. Coop. I wanna take down Mark Fredericks and The Big F, I want people to know why it happened, and I want them to be so fucking scared.

COOPER. That's...gonna take some planning.

BENNETT. But yes?

COOPER. Sure. We can do that.

BENNETT. Good.

> *(He hangs up.* **COOPER** *goes back to stuffing envelopes.)*

BENNETT. Thank you for the good stuff, and there was a lot of good stuff, I love you, goodbye.

> *(He leaves. The spotlight blacks out.* **MUSGROVE** *enters with a baby bag, carrying takeout from Chick-fil-A.)*

MUSGROVE. Look at my superstar volunteer, back already. Thomas, we're gonna have to put you on the payroll.

COOPER. Just doing my part, Mrs. Musgrove. How was Reverend Orton's funeral?

MUSGROVE. Oh, I didn't go. But I sent a note to his wife, and a plant.

COOPER. Well, that was very thoughtful.

MUSGROVE. Do you think I should have gone?

COOPER. Ethically or politically?

MUSGROVE. I used to think those were not mutually exclusive. But...it's a means to an end.

COOPER. Of course. Oh, Mrs. Musgrove, I meant to ask you, do you know anything about the singles events at the Faith and Family Foundation?

MUSGROVE. Not a lot, but I know it's a pretty active group – I think they even have a bowling league. You mean some girl hasn't already snatched you up?

COOPER. I have managed to avoid...snatching.

MUSGROVE. Well, when would they have the chance? You work too much. Tell you what we'll do, we'll go right to the source. Mark Fredericks is a dear friend of the family.

COOPER. Is he? I had no idea.

> *(***PRESTON*** *enters.* **COOPER** *distracts himself with paperwork.)*

PRESTON. Peggy.

MUSGROVE. Deirdre, good to see you.

PRESTON. Thanks for making some time for me.

MUSGROVE. Of course! Deirdre Preston, this is Thomas Harlow, one of my best volunteers.

COOPER. It's an honor to meet you.

PRESTON. Thomas, you look so familiar, have we met before?

COOPER. Oh, golly. I'd remember if we had.

MUSGROVE. Why don't we step into my office? Thomas, coffee?

COOPER. Yes ma'am.

(The ladies depart as lights fade.)

Scene Seventeen

(Cooper and Bennett's house. **BENNETT** *is packing a suitcase from the contents of a laundry basket.* **ADAM** *is at hand, wearing a jacket.)*

ADAM. But why run off to Alabama? Is it Mardi Gras already?

BENNETT. I just... I said my goodbye. I don't wanna be here when it happens. I keep thinking of the funeral, and people won't know how they're supposed to treat me, you know? So I wanna be someplace where I don't have to talk about Sammy, or feelings, and my dad's house is perfect for that. A few days of emotional avoidance with the demolition expert and I'll be right as rain.

ADAM. I got you a present. Sort of. To lift your spirits.

(He removes his jacket, revealing a t-shirt prominently featuring Alf.)

Here, kitty kitty.

BENNETT. That's your Alf? Your Alf is terrible.

ADAM. Alf is quite possibly the worst thing I've ever seen. When's the last time you watched that show?

BENNETT. And yet you got yourself a t-shirt.

ADAM. I *made* myself a t-shirt. To remind us that nostalgia isn't what it used to be. The future. That's where the good stuff is.

BENNETT. I like to think so.

ADAM. Go home. Fill up on Alabama carbs. Kimberly and I will cover for ya. Come back, things will be different. Maybe not better, but different, which is a start. Wanna do Pride stuff this weekend?

BENNETT. I'm sorry?

ADAM. It's Pride weekend. The parade, all that? We've got the free time. Allison's not doing much since she's trying to downplay the activism.

BENNETT. I completely forgot it's Pride weekend. It's so fucked up Atlanta has it in October.

ADAM. That's our gay Atlanta. Well-intentioned, but always a little late for the party.

BENNETT. Yes. I will absolutely be back for Pride. What time you got?

ADAM. A little after six, you better hit the road. You used to wear a watch.

BENNETT. I left it someplace.

ADAM. Here.

> *(Removing his own.)*

Take mine.

BENNETT. I'm not gonna take your watch. I lose things, we just established that.

ADAM. I trust you. Plus, if I keep it I'll just be counting the hours 'til you come back.

BENNETT. I love how sincerely cheesy you are. You're really awesome. Thank you for being awesome.

ADAM. *No problem.*

BENNETT. Still terrible.

> *(Lights fade.)*

Scene Eighteen

(The media wall comes to life. A campaign ad. Images of **HAINES** *as grand marshal of a pride parade, followed by footage of dancing male strippers on rainbow floats, topless women on motorcycles with black censor bars over their chests, drag queens, and same-sex couples kissing.)*

NARRATOR. *(Voice-over.)* Senator Allison Haines claims she represents everyone in her district. But who is the real Allison Haines? Last year, she served as grand marshal of a gay pride parade. She has made personal donations to radical activist groups like the ACLU. Who does Senator Haines actually represent?

*(***MARK FREDERICKS**, *addressing the camera.)*

FREDERICKS. Hi, I'm Mark Fredericks, of the Faith and Family Foundation. My friend Peggy Musgrove is running to represent your community, your *values*, and your concerns. Let's help her get to work.

(The media wall goes dark. The house, days later. **BENNETT** *and* **COOPER** *are in the kitchen, packing a picnic basket.)*

BENNETT. What kind of cheese is this?

COOPER. Lorraine.

BENNETT. Never heard of it.

COOPER. It's kind of like a mild Swiss.

BENNETT. I don't care for Swiss.

COOPER. That's why I didn't get Swiss. I got Lorraine.

BENNETT. How's it different?

COOPER. It's different in that it is not Swiss.

BENNETT. I'm suspicious.

COOPER. No one's gonna make you eat it. You can sit there and munch on those pistachios you're suddenly so obsessed with.

BENNETT. They keep my hands busy. Distract me from wanting a cigarette.

COOPER. How compelling that you must always have a filthy habit of some kind.

(Doorbell.)

BENNETT. Doorbell.

COOPER. Oh, really, is that what that was?

BENNETT. Are you expecting anyone?

COOPER. You cannot be serious.

*(**BENNETT** looks out the peephole.)*

BENNETT. Go to your room.

COOPER. Is it your fucking boyfriend? We agreed –

BENNETT. It's not Adam – it's Kimberly. Go, I'll get rid of her.

COOPER. Hurry.

*(**COOPER** exits to hall.)*

BENNETT. And he is not my boyfriend!

(He opens the door.)

Kimberly. Hey.

KIMBERLY. Hey, I'm sorry to bother you at home. Do you have a moment?

BENNETT. Um, sure. Sure. I'm actually just on my way out, but I've got a couple minutes.

*(**KIMBERLY** enters. Nervous.)*

KIMBERLY. I won't stay long, I've gotta go pick up the kids at day care. Is Cooper home?

BENNETT. He is, but he's taking a nap.

KIMBERLY. How was Alabama?

BENNETT. Oh, well. It's my dad. You pretty much know what you're getting before you get there, and he doesn't disappoint. How was the memorial?

KIMBERLY. They didn't mention the last twelve years of his life. Gave him a total rewrite. Awful. But then, after his parents tried to de-gay his existence at the funeral, the procession had to drive past the setup for the Pride parade. So there were all these male strippers stapling fabric to trailers, and the guys from the Eagle took off their biker hats as a show of respect. Sammy would have... Sammy would have loved it...

BENNETT. You okay?

KIMBERLY. I'm – not sure. Haines wanted your notes on the penny tax for public schools, and I figured since you weren't at the service I shouldn't bother you.

BENNETT. Why didn't you just say so? Gimme your thumb drive.

KIMBERLY. No, this was hours ago. You know how she is, she wanted it right that minute. I used remote access on your laptop, I figured I could find the file.

BENNETT. Ah.

KIMBERLY. I was not snooping. Everything was just open on your desktop.

BENNETT. What was, Kimberly? What do you think you saw?

KIMBERLY. Some pretty extensive notes on how to work with nitroglycerin.

BENNETT. Yes. My father works in demolition. I'm learning about the family business so we have something to talk about. It's as dull as it sounds.

KIMBERLY. You didn't clear your web history, Bennett. The week before Lucas Orton died, you looked up the sites for the Aqua club, you researched chloroform. There was a fucking PowerPoint presentation.

BENNETT. You still going with that story about not snooping, or have we moved past that?

KIMBERLY. I...don't know what's happening here.

BENNETT. That's a good place to be. Don't you want to stay there?

KIMBERLY. I want to know why you have the floor plan for the Faith and Family Foundation.

BENNETT. It's available on their website. Anyone can pull that up.

KIMBERLY. Why do you have it?

COOPER. *(Entering.)* That was me. I'm fascinated by architecture. The Faith and Family Foundation has done marvels with cinder blocks and linoleum.

BENNETT. I thought you were napping.

COOPER. I woke up. Something startled me.

KIMBERLY. Am I discussing this with both of you?

COOPER. If we're discussing this at all. Because right now you have questions and suspicions, but you don't have answers. How prepared are you for what happens after you have answers?

BENNETT. Coop, stop it.

KIMBERLY. Maybe I should go.

BENNETT. No, stay. We should talk.

COOPER. I'm sorry, I thought we had somewhere to be. We're going on a picnic, and then we're going to Piedmont Park to buy some rainbow-striped crap.

> *(***KIMBERLY*** *starts for the door.)*

BENNETT. No, Kimberly –

> *(***BENNETT*** *blocks her exit.* ***COOPER*** *goes to the picnic basket.)*

KIMBERLY. I shouldn't have come here.

BENNETT. I really wish you hadn't.

KIMBERLY. Bennett. Listen to me. They keep a registry of everyone who buys hazardous chemicals, so if questions come up –

BENNETT. Lucas Orton is in the ground. No one is questioning how he died because they're so distracted by how he lived.

KIMBERLY. The things that you're doing, whatever you're planning. I stumbled across it by accident. How long do you think it'll take someone who's actually looking for it? You're going to get caught.

BENNETT. No. We're not.

KIMBERLY. Just listen to me! I've worked with you every day for three years, you're my friend, my children love you. You're good, and kind, this is not in your nature –

BENNETT. Goddamn it, what do we have to do for people to see us as a credible threat? For fuck's sake, I am a *man*! I killed Lucas Orton with my bare fucking hands! What does it take? Huh?

KIMBERLY. No no no –

COOPER. Bennett! Stop it. It's alright. Kimberly. I'm pointing a gun at you right now, and if you try to leave, I'm going to shoot you. Do you believe me?

KIMBERLY. ...Yes.

BENNETT. Sorry.

> (**COOPER** *tosses the backpack across the room.*)

COOPER. There's zip ties and duct tape in the front pocket.

BENNETT. Kimberly, can you get those out for me?

KIMBERLY. Bennett. Just stop and think. You're in control here, Bennett. You have the power to stop it. I'm depending on your strength, Bennett, you can still do what's right.

BENNETT. Yes, Kimberly. That's what I'm trying to do, *Kimberly*. And I'm a writer, *Kimberly*, so there's no need to try and diffuse the situation through the repeated use of my name, *Kimberly*.

COOPER. Bennett, you've gotta take it down a notch.

BENNETT. She never should have come here! Why did you do that? Why did you have to come here?

KIMBERLY. I'm your friend.

BENNETT. I know that don't you think I know that?

> (**KIMBERLY** *turns around, facing* **COOPER** *and the gun.*)

KIMBERLY. I told my husband I was coming over. He'll come looking for me.

COOPER. Don't lie. Even if you told him you were coming over, you didn't tell him why.

BENNETT. *(Checks his watch.)* We're running out of time.

KIMBERLY. For what?

COOPER. A picnic, I told you.

BENNETT. I think she'd be more comfortable on my bed.

COOPER. Yeah. Okay.

> *(**KIMBERLY** looks at each of them. She picks up the backpack and heads for the hall. **COOPER** follows. **BENNETT** goes to the kitchen, opens a cabinet, removes the bottle of chloroform, takes a dish towel, and exits down the hall as everything goes dark.)*

Scene Nineteen

KIMBERLY. *(Voice-over.)* You've reached the voicemail of Kimberly Phillips, please leave a message.

> *(Beep.)*

DAYCARE WORKER. *(Voice-over.)* Mrs. Phillips, this is Katie at Decatur First Day School. Ava and Stephanie were scheduled for five-thirty pickup. Please be advised our rate is five dollars per minute after five forty-five.

> *(The explosion from Scene One is heard.)*
>
> *(Beep.)*

KIMBERLY'S HUSBAND. *(Voice-over.)* Hey babe, I'm stuck on two-eighty-five, there's a...big fire, something. Hey, was I supposed to pick up the girls, because, um – they called, so...call me.

> *(Beep.)*

HAINES. *(Voice-over.)* Kimberly. Allison Haines. Are you watching the news? Call me. Now.

> *(Beep.)*

KIMBERLY'S HUSBAND. *(Voice-over.)* Kim, hey. I've, ah, got the girls. We're just wondering what's up. Seriously. Call me.

> *(Beep.)*
>
> *(Twilight. We hear movement from the hallway and, slowly, we see the figure of* **KIMBERLY** *crawling on. She's been gagged with a bandana, her hands and feet are bound with zip ties, and torn duct tape is at her wrists, ankles, and midsection. She makes it to the door, but sees the deadbolt requires a key from the inside. New plan. Over to the floor lamp, and then inching her way to the window. She loses her grip. The lamp falls. As she tries to retrieve it, we hear the key in the lock, and the door opens.* **COOPER** *is in first.*

He sees the lamp and motions for **BENNETT** *to stay back.* **BENNETT** *takes the gun from the picnic basket, then searches the room with his phone flashlight.* **COOPER** *removes something from his pocket. The light lands on* **KIMBERLY**, *bound on the floor.* **COOPER** *walks over. We see a laser dot on her body, then see the flash and hear the sudden jolt of the taser in* **COOPER**'s *hand.* **KIMBERLY** *slumps to the floor. The two of them move her to the sofa.* **COOPER** *exits.)*

(Time passes. Night falls. **BENNETT** *sits on the kitchen counter, smoking.* **KIMBERLY** *stirs. She looks at* **BENNETT**.*)*

BENNETT. I know, I know, but it's been a hell of a day, and I'm only having one.

(He walks over to her.)

I'm going to remove the gag.

(She nods. He takes the bandana off. She gasps for air.)

KIMBERLY. Water.

BENNETT. Oh, sure.

(He goes to the kitchen, gets bottled water from the fridge. Finds a straw. He brings it back and helps her sit up. He serves her the water.)

We bombed The Big F. Mark Fredericks is dead.

KIMBERLY. Oh my god.

BENNETT. We tried to localize it to one small area, his little smoking spot, but we overdid it. We're new to all this. We followed the same model Timothy McVeigh used in Oklahoma City, only we tied it into the gas main as an accelerant. It pretty much took out the whole building.

KIMBERLY. More than just Mark Fredericks?

BENNETT. Oh, yeah. And part of me hates that, but then I think, well, they were working there, right?

KIMBERLY. Bennett, those were secretaries and janitors. They never did anything to you.

BENNETT. Tell me, Kimberly, how far down the Nazi chain of command do you have to go before you get to the people who were just doing their jobs? Hitler, evil. Himmler, Goebbels, evil, evil. Their drivers, maybe? It's assigning nuance to a nightmare. Those people are casualties of a war we didn't start. We're fighting back, and you're gonna feel bad for *them*?

KIMBERLY. I don't feel bad for them, Bennett. But I worry for you because I care about you.

BENNETT. I need you to understand that we are not going to stop. And the problem I can't get past is, I don't think you'll be able to sit quietly while that happens.

KIMBERLY. I want you to stop, because there's a chance if you do, you might not spend the rest of your life in jail. Hell, you and Cooper could leave town. We'll get you money – Daniel and I have over twenty thousand saved up for a house, we'll go to the bank on Monday –

BENNETT. Jesus, Kimberly, I'm not gonna take your house money. And why would we leave town right when we're finally starting to make a difference?

> (**COOPER** *enters through the front door, locks it behind him. He carries various rainbow-striped paraphernalia.*)

COOPER. Sorry, I didn't mean to be so long. I went to Blake's, kept telling people you were in the bathroom. Wandered around the park, acted really drunk, hugged everybody I halfway knew. Alibi accomplished. And look who's up.

KIMBERLY. Cooper. Bennett. I just want to go home to Danny, and Ava, and Stephanie. I will do whatever you need me to do, but please. Let me go home.

BENNETT. Kimberly, I swear to God I'm trying to figure out how to let you do that.

KIMBERLY. I won't say anything. I won't!

COOPER. Shh! Bennett, may I see you in the kitchen, please?

*(***COOPER*** and ***BENNETT*** go to the kitchen.)*

BENNETT. I really think she won't tell.

COOPER. For how long? You know what's coming next. You really think she'll keep quiet? She's not gonna stay afraid. She'll get police protection, and that'll be the end of it. And she won't even do it out of spite, she'll do it because she thinks it's all morally fucking correct.

BENNETT. I'm gonna be sick.

COOPER. No you're not. Cowboy up.

*(***BENNETT*** walks over to ***KIMBERLY***.)*

BENNETT. Focus on me. You're not leaving. You can't. I wish you could. But you can't. This has nothing to do with you or me, do you understand that?

(She spits in his face.)

COOPER. Turn on some music.

*(***COOPER*** exits to the hall.)*

KIMBERLY. My girls. They need to know they're fucking brilliant and they're the only thing I ever really got right, and no matter what, they've got to finish college. They can do whatever they want after, but they've got to get that piece of paper or it just fucks your life.

BENNETT. Okay.

KIMBERLY. And you're so right about having to live with bad tattoos, I have a ying-yang on my shoulder, I don't even know why I got it, I hate it so much, don't let them get tattoos at nineteen, you can't undo it.

You make sure Danny knows I said that, please, please. I don't care how, you're a great liar, you can come up with something, maybe I said it over lunch one day before you fucking murdered me you son of a bitch! NOTHING IS WORTH THIS!

*(***COOPER*** comes running in, holding chloroform and a towel.)*

COOPER. What the fuck! Shut up!

KIMBERLY. HEEEEEEELP! Please, I'm begging you. Bennett! Stop this! Please!

> (**COOPER** *runs over to the iPod dock, turns it on, loud. It's something horribly incongruous – the synth-heavy remix of an autotuned chanteuse.**)

COOPER. Just go to the fucking kitchen!

> (**BENNETT** *can't move.* **COOPER** *carefully opens the bottle and pours onto the towel.* **KIMBERLY** *lets out a primal wail. She fights back, hard.*)
>
> (**COOPER** *grabs a throw pillow from the sofa and straddles her, throwing the towel over her face and then holding the pillow over it, pressing both into her face.*)

BENNETT. *(Finding his voice.)* Cooper! Stop!

> (*But she's stopped moving.* **COOPER** *slides off of her, sweating, panting.* **BENNETT** *lets a sob escape. It's done. They lift her body and take it down the hall as lights fade.*)

---

*A license to produce *Angry Fags* does not include a performance license for any third-party or copyrighted music. Licensees should create an original composition or use music in the public domain. For further information, please see Music Use Note on page 3.

Scene Twenty

(Haines's office. **HAINES** *pacing.* **PRESTON** *is seated.)*

PRESTON. Allison, I came to you as a courtesy. You've got a dead campaign staffer and a missing person's report for your office manager. People are going to expect answers.

HAINES. And Deirdre, I swear to god if I had answers I'd tell you. For god's sake, the Faith and Family Foundation just got bombed yesterday, we've got two hundred fifty thousand people in town for a cancelled Pride parade, isn't there anything else you could be focusing on right now?

PRESTON. Right now, this is my focus. Is it possible Kimberly Phillips needed a break for a few days?

HAINES. This is not some runaway mommy. I know my people.

PRESTON. Do you know that Bennett Riggs' roommate is volunteering on the Peggy Musgrove campaign?

HAINES. Cooper? You must be mistaken. Aside from the ideological differences, it would be completely out of character for Cooper to volunteer for anything.

PRESTON. He was one of the witnesses who gave a description of Samuel Garrison's assailant. I saw him with you at the police station that morning. I read his statement. And then earlier this week, I ran into him, working at Musgrove's office. Of course, he has every right to volunteer for Peggy Musgrove. I'm just wondering why he is. And I'm wondering if you know your people as well as you think you do.

(Lights fade.)

Scene Twenty-One

(**BENNETT** *and* **COOPER**, *on a park bench. There's a bag from McDonald's between them, and they're holding drinks. The mood is somber.*)

COOPER. I ordered a McRib, because I heard it was back. But they didn't have it. I asked if they were just out temporarily or if I'd missed my window of opportunity altogether. She couldn't give me any concrete answers.

BENNETT. People always want what they can't have.

(*He sips his soda.*)

The police called. Adam told them that Kimberly remoted into my computer, so they'd like me to bring it in. In case she did any web searches, something.

COOPER. I see.

BENNETT. But my backpack was stolen yesterday, when we were at Pride.

COOPER. Oh, that's right, I forgot.

BENNETT. I think we should stop.

COOPER. If we stop now, nothing changes. It was just a random series of events. If we stop now, everything we've done was pointless. It means Sammy died for nothing. It means Kimberly died for nothing.

BENNETT. Are you scared?

COOPER. Yes. I am. That's how I know it matters.

BENNETT. But the odds of getting caught –

COOPER. Bennett. Stop pretending. They are going to catch us. At this point we're just seeing what we can accomplish before they do.

BENNETT. Yeah.

(*He sips.*)

God, now I really want a McRib.

COOPER. That's how they get you.

(*They sip their sodas as lights fade.*)

Scene Twenty-Two

(Musgrove's office, a few hours later. **MUSGROVE** *is working at her desk.* **COOPER** *enters.)*

COOPER. Mrs. Musgrove?

MUSGROVE. Thomas. I didn't realize anyone was still here. It's late, you should go home.

COOPER. I'm just trying to keep busy. If I go online, turn on the TV, it's all so awful. The police announced it wasn't a gas explosion. It was definitely a bomb.

MUSGROVE. I know. But I already knew. This was no accident. We are under siege, Thomas.

COOPER. Fox News said it's no coincidence that it happened during the whole Gay Pride thing. There's fights all over Midtown.

MUSGROVE. Nothing good will come from that.

COOPER. I just don't understand who would do something like this.

MUSGROVE. That's the thing about terrorists. They don't think like you and me. They're so blinded by hatred, it's all they know.

COOPER. But it starts somewhere, right?

MUSGROVE. Well, yes. It started with Original Sin. I believe that there is evil in this world, and the challenge God puts before us is fighting that evil with everything we've got.

COOPER. What are you working on?

MUSGROVE. I'm writing an editorial, remembering Mark Fredericks. It's hard to write this sort of thing without it all sounding so Hallmark, you know?

COOPER. Want me to take a look?

MUSGROVE. Thank you. Yes, I could use another set of eyes on it.

(She passes him a few papers, then turns to her laptop as he reads. **COOPER** *reads silently*

as lights rise on Haines's house. **HAINES** *enters, followed by* **BENNETT.***)*

HAINES. You'd think by now they'd at least find her car. God. I know something's happened to her, Bennett.

BENNETT. Maybe not, Senator. There's no reason to assume the worst.

HAINES. Then why the hell wouldn't she call someone? Leave a note? Something.

BENNETT. I really don't know. Where's your family?

HAINES. Marilyn took the kids to my mom's. Just to get them away from all the insanity.

COOPER. This is really good, Mrs. Musgrove.

MUSGROVE. Thomas, at this point I think you can call me Peggy.

COOPER. Yes ma'am. Peggy. It's good. From the heart, but restrained, respectful.

HAINES. Bennett. This is going to be a difficult conversation.

BENNETT. I hate conversations that start like that.

HAINES. It's come to my attention that Cooper is working for Peggy Musgrove, and I think you know that.

BENNETT. I did not know that.

HAINES. Don't lie to me, Bennett. Why's he there?

BENNETT. It's nothing nefarious. He's got a crush on a Log Cabin Republican. His name's David.

HAINES. Jesus. I could face the state election board on this – it looks like I've got a goddamn spy in the Musgrove campaign. This is the last thing I need when we're recovering from sixty innocent people getting blown up at The Big F.

BENNETT. Why does everyone keep saying that? They were fighting equality and women's reproductive rights! I still don't understand why we cancelled the parade for them – they were the enemy!

HAINES. Terrorism is not a means to any solution.

BENNETT. It's only terrorism if it doesn't work. When it works, we call it a revolution.

(**HAINES** *studies* **BENNETT** *for a long moment.*)

COOPER. I made a couple of notes, but it's just little stuff. You honor him beautifully, ma'am.

MUSGROVE. Thank you, Thomas.

COOPER. I should get home.

> (**COOPER** *rises, and* **MUSGROVE** *shakes his hand over the desk.* **HAINES** *rises.* **COOPER** *heads for the door.*)

HAINES. You haven't had time to deal with Sammy. And now Kimberly. I think you need to step back and plan your next move. I'm sorry, Bennett. But if anyone finds out about Cooper in Musgrove's office, I can't have you on my payroll.

COOPER. Peggy? This may sound so stupid, but...

BENNETT. Are you firing me?

COOPER. Could I have a hug?

HAINES. No. You're resigning.

MUSGROVE. Of course.

BENNETT. Of course. You'll need my security badge.

> (**MUSGROVE** *crosses around her desk to* **COOPER** *as* **BENNETT** *takes the taser from his pocket and fires. The sound of the taser is heard as* **COOPER** *receives* **MUSGROVE**'s *embrace.* **HAINES** *cries out and falls.* **BENNETT** *removes a zip tie from his pocket and binds her hands.*)

MUSGROVE. I promise. Everything's going to be better soon.

COOPER. I believe that. I really do.

> (**COOPER** *exits as lights fade.*)

Scene Twenty-Three

*(In the darkness, a cell phone rings. Lights up on **ADAM** as he answers.)*

ADAM. Hey.

*(Lights up on **BENNETT**.)*

BENNETT. Hey. What are you doing?

ADAM. TV. Nothing. Trying to turn my brain off. Come over.

BENNETT. I can't. I'm waiting on Cooper, we've got plans.

ADAM. Can you cancel?

BENNETT. No, it's too late for that. Just talk to me.

ADAM. About what?

BENNETT. Anything. What're you watching?

ADAM. I was watching the news. All the networks are reporting live from The Big F. Awful stuff, you know? And then my DVR pops up and says, "You are scheduled to record *Iron Chef America*. Change the channel?" And I gave in. Just take me away, you know? It'll all be there in an hour.

BENNETT. What's the ingredient?

ADAM. Apples.

BENNETT. I can't eat raw apples. They make my teeth itch.

ADAM. I've never heard of that. Is that like an allergy?

BENNETT. Don't know. Never bothered to check.

ADAM. Well you should, it sounds pretty serious. You sure you don't wanna come over?

BENNETT. I want to. But I can't. Adam, do you ever think about how much easier things would be if you'd just stayed on the farm?

ADAM. No. I don't. I feel sorry for them. That kind of isolation, it's just willful ignorance. You can convince yourself everything's fine as long as you don't pay attention. Ooh. He's hollowing out an apple and filling it with risotto. Can you eat *baked* apples?

BENNETT. Yeah.

ADAM. But once you know everything isn't fine, you can't pretend anymore. That's why we do what we do. It's why you learn how the game is played.

BENNETT. It's not a game. It seems like it, but it isn't.

ADAM. Just because the consequences are real for people like us doesn't mean the people in charge aren't playing a game. You probably didn't call to listen to me get on a soapbox.

BENNETT. I called because I wanted to hear you.

ADAM. You're worried about Kimberly.

BENNETT. That's part of it.

ADAM. They'll find her. If they could find the guy who attacked Sammy, they can find Kimberly.

BENNETT. But they still haven't found the guy who attacked Sammy.

ADAM. Yeah they did. The APD told the senator. Jesus, I guess you were in Alabama. I thought you knew.

BENNETT. How do they know they got the right guy?

ADAM. Fingerprints on the baseball bat. I can't believe nobody called you. It's a homicide now. Cooper knows this.

BENNETT. Cooper doesn't know.

ADAM. Sure he does. They made Cooper come in for a lineup, he said he couldn't be sure. But the bartender made a positive ID, and so did your friends, um –

BENNETT. Lance, and his stupid friend Coby.

ADAM. Yeah. My point is, the system works. You just have to have faith in it.

> (**BENNETT** *is thunderstruck.*)

You there? Bennett?

BENNETT. I'm here.

> (*A breath.*)

I'm gonna tell you some stuff, okay?

ADAM. Okay.

BENNETT. And after I do, I'm gonna hang up.

ADAM. Where are you? I'll come to you.

BENNETT. Listen to me. As soon as I'm done, I'm just gonna hang up, because I don't want you to feel obligated to respond to what I say. So before I say anything, I want you to know that I wish the whole world was filled with people like you. I really do.

ADAM. You're sweet.

BENNETT. Do the noise.

ADAM. *Shhhhp.*

BENNETT. Thanks for that. Okay.

> (**BENNETT** *takes a ragged breath of preparation as lights fade.*)

Scene Twenty-Four

*(**HAINES** is on her sofa. Her hands are bound behind her back and there is tape over her mouth. **COOPER** is setting up a video camera.)*

COOPER. You know the real bitch of it all, is that when I voted for you, I felt good about it. Not just because of what Sammy and Bennett said about you, but because I believed *you*. I really thought you'd be an agent for change. So when you failed to deliver, when you turned out to be just like everybody else, it felt like such a fucking betrayal. I mean, Musgrove is a religious nut who thinks God manufactures terrorists to teach us lessons about evil, which is a dick move on God's part if you ask me, but at least she's *consistent*. But people like you promise the moon, and then you get in office and forget everything that you claimed was important.

> *(Calls off.)*

Jesus, Bennett, did you fall in?

> *(Back to **HAINES**.)*

You fired him? Seriously? It's like loyalty doesn't mean anything anymore.

> *(He approaches her.)*

Are you going to stay quiet?

> *(She nods.)*

Don't let me down here.

> *(**COOPER** removes the tape from her mouth.)*

HAINES. Cooper, whatever you're planning –

COOPER. Fox News is blaming left-wing extremists for the attack on The Big F. Which is good, because for once, they're correct. Bound to happen once, right? Monkeys at a typewriter and all that. The thought is, it's one thing to say *the gays* are ruining your life because they're making you sell them cake, but it's another to actually accuse us of domestic terrorism. So *the gays* are pissed. And in a political movement, timing is everything. This will be our moment, to start acting like we've got a fucking spine. We just need that final push. You can make that happen.

HAINES. Cooper, no matter how horrible Fredericks and his people were, they didn't deserve to be killed. I won't make a statement supporting that.

COOPER. Oh, no no no. You're not going to be our spokesperson. You're going to be our martyr.

HAINES. Oh my God.

COOPER. A movement doesn't really come together until there's a fallen leader. The gay community doesn't have a Martin Luther King. *And don't say Harvey Milk.* Everybody says Harvey Milk! The mayor was straight, and he got killed too. People forget that because Victor Garber played it in the movie and he wasn't A-List, but he's had a really good career. Excuse me a moment. Bennett! What are you *doing* in there?

> (**COOPER** *exits. We hear him banging on a door.* **ADAM** *enters and motions for* **HAINES** *to stay quiet. He hides as* **COOPER** *returns.*)

He's ill. He gets a nervous stomach. Normally I bring Tums. You got any Pepto or anything?

HAINES. Medicine cabinet.

COOPER. Bennett, look in the medicine cabinet!

> (**BENNETT** *enters.*)

BENNETT. I'm fine. Sorry.

HAINES. Bennett, you know this won't solve anything.

BENNETT. It will if we win. Allison, you're going to die tonight, and nothing's going to change that. The option we're giving you is to make a statement, on tape, that people will remember for generations. You can be the face of change. Or you can refuse to do that, and die anyway.

HAINES. I have a family, Bennett.

BENNETT. I know. But you chose to be a public servant, and that takes priority.

COOPER. Would it help if you heard the speech?

(He produces several oversized prints.)

BENNETT. Coop.

COOPER. Just an excerpt. I printed it big so you'd have cue cards. We don't have time for you to memorize.

(He reads.)

"Several years ago, I created a video as part of the 'It Gets Better' campaign in support of LGBT youth. The message was wrong. What I should have said was, it only gets better if you take action. It only gets better if you refuse to compromise, refuse to apologize for taking what is rightfully yours. In order for it to get better, you have to *make* it better."

(Stops.)

It continues in that vein. It's no "I Have a Dream," but it's got a message that sticks. This'll go viral.

BENNETT. Coop, give me the gun, go to her closet, find her something to wear.

COOPER. Do we have a color preference?

BENNETT. She looks good in blue.

*(**COOPER** hands the gun to **BENNETT** and exits. **ADAM** emerges with scissors, cutting the zip ties.)*

Allison, get up.

HAINES. What the hell is going on?

BENNETT. Adam's getting you out of here, just go.

HAINES. Who am I supposed to trust right now?

ADAM. I'm not leaving you behind, Bennett.

HAINES. Then let me go on my own.

ADAM. Calm down. We've got the gun. Allison, you're safe.

*(**COOPER** returns, holding two suits.)*

COOPER. Do we have a favorite?

   (Looks around.)

   Okay, just so I'm clear, were we expecting him?

ADAM. Bennett told me everything.

COOPER. Christ, must we always include whoever you're dating in everything?

BENNETT. We don't have to do this.

COOPER. Why, because Prince Smarmy says we don't? Jesus, that's our friendship, isn't it? We're thick as thieves until you start fucking someone and then that magically gives them power of veto.

BENNETT. Goddamn it Cooper, not everything is a fucking allegory! We have been sloppy, and stupid, and we're going to get caught, you said so yourself.

COOPER. THAT'S WHY WE FINISH IT, YOU COCKSUCKING IDIOT! PROTECT THE FUCKING TRIBE!

BENNETT. Why didn't you tell me they caught the guy who attacked Sammy?

COOPER. I'm not sure they did.

BENNETT. They have his fingerprints on the baseball bat, Cooper.

COOPER. You're just taking everyone's word over mine, aren't you? Sometimes you are a really shitty friend.

BENNETT. You kept it a secret because you knew you got it wrong.

COOPER. I assumed you didn't give a shit, since you were fucking Adam the whole time Sammy was in a goddamn coma!

BENNETT. You started this. You started all of this with your "make it better" murder of *an innocent stranger.*

COOPER. Who murdered Reverend Orton? Who stole a case of nitroglycerin from his shitty father? Who stood there, and did *nothing*, while Kimberly died in our living room?

ADAM. You watched him kill Kimberly?

BENNETT. I couldn't stop it.

ADAM. You didn't say you were there.

COOPER. He drove the car with *her body in the trunk*. He's the planner, he's the manipulator, people just fall for it because he's so goddamn affable. The whole world wants to take care of Bennett Riggs, so he never has to be held accountable for anything! Does Mister Wonderful know our grand plan? About who's taking the fall for Haines's assassination?

   (No one says anything.)

HAINES. Well, I'm certainly curious.

COOPER. It's right-wing extremists, retaliating for The Big F. And Peggy Musgrove is behind the whole thing. She's been sending instructions from her campaign office to a mysterious assassin with a Gmail account? I couldn't come up with this, it takes a fucking writer.

HAINES. Peggy Musgrove is a decent person.

COOPER. Oh shut up.

BENNETT. This is all over. It ends tonight.

ADAM. It can't end. Not like this.

HAINES. What?

ADAM. Look where we are right now. Orton's dead. The Faith and Family Foundation is national news, with an outpouring of support. They managed to shut down the Pride parade. Musgrove comes out looking like a compassionate conservative. You've made liberal terrorism a thing, and that didn't exist before. All you've done is make Allison unelectable, and empowered the other side. We can't leave it like this.

COOPER. Adam, I misjudged you, you're good people.

BENNETT. We could have both been working for Musgrove. She could have masterminded The Big F bombing to try and get sympathy for her cause.

COOPER. Bennett, your plan doesn't work because it requires us to confess. We have to disappear.

BENNETT. You don't get it, do you? We're never going to outrun this. And we don't deserve to. We were wrong! Don't you understand that? We were wrong about everything!

COOPER. Fuck you! I'm not giving up!

BENNETT. I know. I love you.

> (*BENNETT embraces* **COOPER**, *holding him close. He pulls the gun on* **HAINES** *and* **ADAM**, *who recoil.* **BENNETT** *lowers the gun and fires it three times, directly into* **COOPER**'s *side.* **COOPER** *collapses into* **BENNETT**'s *arms and is lowered to the floor.* **BENNETT** *kneels beside him, looks up at* **ADAM**.)

And I love you.

> (**BENNETT** *puts the gun to his head and fires. He falls to the floor.* **HAINES** *screams.*)

HAINES. Oh my god. Oh my god, what have you done?

> (**HAINES** *falls to the floor, sobbing.* **ADAM** *removes gloves from his pocket. He goes to* **BENNETT**'s *body, closes his eyes. He gently removes the gun from* **BENNETT**'s *hand, kisses the hand, lowers it to the floor.* **ADAM** *stands exactly where* **BENNETT** *stood.*)

What do we do?

ADAM. We seize the moment.

> (*He raises the gun. Blackout. Gunshot.*)

Scene Twenty-Five

(Haines's office. **PRESTON** *enters. A small box on the desk. She casually looks through, picks up one of Allison's high heels.* **ADAM** *enters.)*

ADAM. Deirdre Preston.

PRESTON. Mr. Lowell. Is this a good time?

ADAM. Sure. Marilyn wanted Allison's personal stuff, but she's not ready to come by the office yet.

PRESTON. That's kind of you.

ADAM. I still feel like I work for her, you know? I suppose I do, until they fill her seat in the Senate.

PRESTON. I'm sure you already know how well-received our interview was. Picked up by all the national outlets.

ADAM. Yeah, it's kind of everywhere right now, isn't it? I can't stop picturing walking into Allison's living room. There's always that regret. If I'd gotten there ten minutes before, maybe I could have saved her. Saved Bennett. Cooper fooled all of us. I assume Peggy Musgrove still hasn't admitted anything.

PRESTON. No. She maintains her innocence. But the security footage recovered from the Foundation clearly shows Cooper Harlow planting the bomb.

ADAM. And the email exchange between Musgrove and Cooper speaks for itself.

PRESTON. Certainly appears to. I am curious about one thing, I meant to bring it up in the interview, but it honestly slipped my mind.

ADAM. What's that?

PRESTON. Why did Bennett Riggs die wearing a five-hundred dollar wristwatch? Bulova. Rather above his pay grade, don't you think?

ADAM. I couldn't say.

PRESTON. Probably a gift, most likely significant of nothing, but it caught my attention. I tend to notice the odd details. Consequence of my profession, I suppose.

ADAM. I don't know what to tell you.

PRESTON. That's alright. Not every question needs to be asked. You've got an energy, Adam. I think there could be a bright future ahead for you. I hope we'll be able to continue working together.

ADAM. Absolutely, Deirdre. I've got your number.

PRESTON. And I've got yours.

> (**PRESTON** *exits.* **ADAM** *steps into a spotlight, to applause.*)

ADAM. Allison Haines believed in the future of this state. She believed the world isn't getting *smaller*, it's getting *closer*. That possibility still lies within our reach. Her dream is now our responsibility. The first time I saw Allison Haines was when she created a video as part of the "It Gets Better" campaign in support of LGBT youth. What she should have said was... It only gets better if you take action. It only gets better if you refuse to compromise, refuse to apologize for taking what is rightfully yours. In order for it to get better, you have to make it better.

> (*The media wall comes to life. A huge logo reads: "Adam Lowell for State Senate."*)

This is not just my candidacy. This is the dream of Allison Haines, for her own children, for her community, for you, and for me. It is a passion that survives. Peggy Musgrove and her fellow extremists tried to kill that passion. The forces of hatred and intolerance tried to kill that passion. But we will not allow it. Her dream has become a battle cry, and I am willing to answer that call. Stand with me! For this great state, this great country, for the memory of Allison Haines, we will *make it better*!

> (*A crowd goes wild. Lights fade.*)

End of Play